# THE
# FINAL
# GAME

P.S. Harper

WESTBOW
PRESS®
A DIVISION OF THOMAS NELSON
& ZONDERVAN

WestBow Press books may be ordered through booksellers or by contacting:

WestBow Press
A Division of Thomas Nelson & Zondervan
1663 Liberty Drive
Bloomington, IN 47403
www.westbowpress.com
1 (866) 928-1240

Cover Photo Credit - Colt Fetters

ISBN: 978-1-9736-8387-2 (sc)
ISBN: 978-1-9736-8389-6 (hc)
ISBN: 978-1-9736-8388-9 (e)

Library of Congress Control Number: 2020901272

Printed in the United States of America.

WestBow Press rev. date: 02/12/2020

# Contents

# 1
# A Fallen Hero

*Thump thump ... Thump thump ... Thump thump ... Thump thump ...*

It is total darkness, and there is a deafening, rhythmic sound floating through the night air.

*Thump thump ... Thump thump ... Thump thump ...*

The deep, pounding sound of Jaxon's heartbeat is the only thing he hears, but he is uncertain what the noise is or where it is coming from.

*Thump thump ... Thump thump ... Thump thump ...*

As his heartbeat slightly calms down, he begins to comprehend what the seemingly far-off, beating sound is. He also begins to feel it in his throat.

*Thump thump ... Thump thump ... Thump thump ...*

There are several different, massive banners around the football stadium, campus, and town that show the impressive physique and accolades of college football's most decorated athlete of all time. One banner shows a muscular player, shirtless, surrounded by three Heisman Trophies. The banner reads, *Heisman BULL ... X4?*

There is another banner that shows the extraordinary athlete with his head down and face hidden. He was wearing his now-iconic number eighty-nine jersey, which he wears because of Ephesians 2:8–9. The caption on this banner ironically says, "HumBULL" and shows some of his most impressive statistics:

"Freshman Year: 10 sacks, 9 interceptions (4 returned for touchdowns), 21 tackles for loss, 5 kicks returned for touchdowns, 5 forced fumbles and recovery (4 touchdowns), 2 passing touchdowns. National Awards: Multiple defensive awards, special teams award—Heisman Trophy Winner!

Sophomore Year: 12 sacks, 5 interceptions (4 returned for touchdowns), 23 tackles for loss, 6 kicks returned for touchdowns, 7 forced fumbles and recovery (5 touchdowns), 3 rushing touchdowns, 1 passing touchdown. National Awards: Multiple defensive awards, special teams award—Heisman Trophy Winner (X2)!!

Junior Year: 19 sacks (6 in one game), 14 interceptions (2 returned for touchdowns), 25 tackles for loss, 8 kicks returned for touchdowns, 8 forced fumbles and recovery (3 touchdowns), 5 rushing touchdowns, 1 passing touchdown. National Awards: Multiple defensive awards, special teams award—Heisman Trophy Winner (X3)!!!"

The third and final of the banners and billboards seen throughout the state shows the Mississippi native flexing his rock-hard biceps with the word *UnstoppaBULL!* written across the top. The impressive artwork shows all the player's trophies including three Heisman Trophies and two national championship trophies. Written at the bottom of the marketing piece are the words *Senior Year—Fourth Heisman? First Pick in the NFL Draft? Future NFL Hall of Fame? —UndeniaBULL!*

After making the tackle, the six-foot, five-inch, 260-pound megastar defensive end, who runs an unbelievable 4.4 in the forty-yard dash, is lying lifelessly on his back on his home football field. It is the fourth quarter of his last home college game, and the crowd went deathly silent. Even as an opposing fan, no one never wants there to be a complete lack of sound at a sporting event due to an injury.

He is sweating profusely as he lays motionless beneath the immense lights above. He is wearing his beautiful and perfectly shined black helmet. His bloodred jersey is quickly rising and falling with each breath he fights to take. The crowd went from an enormous roar to instant stillness. This almost always means something bad.

No one can see his face, but the confusion is heard in the raspy, old voice of the television announcer; he is trying to figure out what is going on. "I'm not sure who it is yet, but someone isn't getting up. Who is that? Can anyone see who that is? Can any of you see a number?"

Jaxon Bull, also known as "The Bull," is the complete athlete every little boy wants to be. For that matter, he's the type of man every adult male wants to be. He is the Zeus of college football. There have been many comparisons, but has there really ever been another like him?

The announcer seems to be asking a question more than telling his audience what is going on. He is completely stunned, just like the rest of America. The entire nation is at a standstill. Nobody knows what is happening. His teammates immediately recognize that something is seriously wrong. One by one, shouts of "Trainer!" stream across the field to the sidelines.

As the players, coaches, and fans stare in anticipation of what will happen next, Jaxon continues to lie on the ground, not moving a muscle.

"I think that's Jaxon Bull. I can't tell if he's moving or not. Did he land on his neck or his head? Boy, you hate to see anyone not get up." The television announcer is still confused. "Let's check the replay."

Jaxon was wearing a pair of dirty, old blue jeans with holes in the knees, but not wearing shoes or shirt, when he was playing in the living room, as a three-year-old ball of energy does, while his dad, Tim, watched football. At least Tim tried to watch football. He had so much fun interacting with his son that he mostly just caught glimpses of the game he loves.

It was on that day that Tim first become an accomplice in his son's taking a self-beating due to Jaxon's adventurous spirit.

"*Wait!*" Tim shouted just before Jaxon leaped from the backside of the couch toward his unsuspecting father. Tim had turned to see a replay of the game when Jaxon decided to perform the maneuver that usually got them both in trouble by Jaxon's mother, who was in the nearby kitchen, preparing dinner.

This had become a normal practice in the Bulls' residence. Jaxon climbed on a piece of furniture in the house and leaped into the air anytime his dad drew near. Each time Jaxon expected his always-reliable father to catch him, no matter what. In his eyes, his dad was the biggest and strongest man in the world. To Jaxon, he was Superman.

Jaxon had been jumping from the seat area of the couch, his dad catching him every time. But Tim looked back toward the television, walking away from the couch when Jaxon made another leap. Jaxon hadn't been paying attention and didn't realize his father had moved from his usual spot. Tim was too far away to make the catch.

It seemed to Tim that Jaxon paused in midair for minutes. Tim lunged toward his airborne son, but he was too late. He wasn't even close.

*Whack!*

Tim heard the smack of Jaxon's head hitting the wood floor, followed by the breath being forced from his tiny, delicate lungs. Jaxon's head whipped backward, and his limp body became instantly lifeless. There were no sounds of crying, and the usual sound of laughter was missing from the room.

Amanda, Jaxon's mother, took notice. After the loud thud, she stopped what she was doing, perked up, and calmly but quickly asked, "What was that?"

Without answering, Tim slid across the living room floor, like a runner sliding feetfirst into second base. Quickly he scooped up his son and firmly held him in his arms. "You're okay! You're fine!" was what immediately came from his panicked father's mouth.

Jaxon was terrifyingly quiet. His eyes were closed, his body unresponsive and hot. Tim began to panic and slightly shook his tiny son as he sternly and quietly said, "Wake up, Son! Wake up! You're okay!"

Tim rocked his son back and forth, trying to wake him up.

Amanda left the kitchen to investigate what was going on in the living room. As she rounded the corner, still drying her hands with the dish rag, she saw Tim on his knees by the coffee table. She could see only Tim's back and Jaxon's feet. She lightheartedly asked, "What are y'all doin' in here? What did you break this time? Which one of y'all am I gonna have to whip?"

As Tim slightly turned his head toward his shoulder, peeking over at his beautiful, young wife, he said, "He hit his head." Upon hearing that, Amanda quickly made her way toward the two culprits. While those words came out of Tim's mouth, Jaxon's eyes slowly began to open.

By the time Amanda got to Jaxon, she could see that his eyes were open. She never realized he had been unconscious. Because he wasn't crying, she assumed he must not be injured. She reached down and started gently rubbing his head, checking for bumps or gashes. She asked Tim, "Is he hurt?"

Before Tim was able to answer, Amanda looked down at her son and asked him, "Are you okay, Jax?"

Upon realizing that Jaxon's eyes were open and that he was conscious but still not crying, Tim looked at his son in astonishment.

Jaxon never raised his head but just slightly smiled at his mother.

She asked again, "Baby, are you hurt?"

Jaxon, never even shedding one tear, raised his head from his father's arms and said, "Uh-huh. I hit my head," with a bigger smile on his face.

"Where did you hit your head?"

Jaxon pointed to a red and slightly swollen spot on his temple.

"Do you want Momma to kiss it?"

Jaxon, still in his father's arms, shifted toward his adoring mother and with a smile on his face said, "Uh-huh," one more time to receive the best medicine a child can receive.

His mother dropped to her knees beside her husband. Tim was still sitting on the floor, stunned by the calmness his son was displaying throughout the whole ordeal. She gently and lovingly rubbed the bump and pressed her soft lips against Jaxon's forehead. From her knees, she sat up straight with perfect posture like a model in a magazine and said, "Y'all please be careful. Don't get hurt and don't break anything, especially bones. You need to stop playing so rough." She then gave Tim a stern look, as if to say, *Stop letting him jump off stuff!*

Amanda stood to her feet, slowly left the room, and went back to what she had been doing in the kitchen. Tim, cautiously watched Amanda leave the room, smiled and saluted to her while saying, "Yes ma'am!"

After she was out of sight, Tim quickly turned his eyes back to his son, with a lot of confusion on his face, and began to wonder, *Was he faking?* He knew his kid was tough. He had seen him bang himself up many times before and always kept going, but this was different. He most certainly knocked himself unconscious.

"Boy, are you okay?" he questioned his son.

"Yeah, Daddy, but my head huwts."

"I reckon it does. You just headbutted the table from the couch. Do you remember doing that?"

Jaxon took a long look at the couch from where he was, then slowly turned his eyes back up toward his father. He shook his head, indicating he had no recollection of what had happened.

"Well, stand up, and let's get a good look at ya. We need to see how messed up ya are. If you're broke, I might need to trade ya in."

With the help of his father, Jaxon slowly stood to his feet and stared into his dad's eyes. "I'm tough!" he said.

A large smile came across Tim's face, and he responded to his son's bravery with, "Tougher than me, boy. You are tougher than me for sure. We're most assuredly gonna have to teach you to make some better choices though. Tough will only get you so far. You've gotta be smart, too!"

It was like that the entire time Jaxon was growing up. When he got hurt, Tim either got the blame or did his best to hide the injury from Amanda. They had a lot of fun in their small hometown of Tishomingo, Mississippi. With Tim and Amanda being such young parents, they were still very spirited and energetic. Jaxon was loaded with scars by the time he was in college. His mom called them "scars," but his dad always called them "lessons."

To Jaxon, Tim was a fun hero of a dad, who was full of great life lessons and wisdom. Amanda was a perfect, nurturing mother who uncompromisingly instilled love and compassion. Tim and Amanda complemented each other extremely well and loved Jaxon with all their hearts. Both parents had to work tremendously hard to make ends meet, but they always made time to be good parents to their only son. It didn't matter whether it was a school play or a Little League baseball game; either Tim or Amanda was there, and usually they were both present and involved.

# 2
# Family History

"He doesn't seem to be moving … The Bull seems to be hurt," the distinct voice of the television announcer explains to the national audience. As Jaxon lies helplessly on the ground, the entire crowd is now silent.

There is one lone figure standing in the crowd. He is slightly taller than those around him. He is older now, but he is nowhere near as old as he appears. The difficult moments he has faced in life, along with all his arduous work out in the elements, have aged this strong man not only in appearance but also in wisdom, patience, and experience.

He is the only one in the stands who currently knows for certain who is on the ground. There isn't a doubt in his soul. He too felt the enormous hit right when Jaxon went to the ground.

Jaxon's dad, Tim "Bulldozer" Bull, married his beautiful childhood sweetheart, Amanda, as soon as they graduated from high school. He was just a rough kid trying to raise a rough kid the best way he knew how. Tim and Amanda started dating when they were both in the eighth grade. Tim was a great athlete in high school and was recruited by every Southeastern Conference (SEC) school to play baseball or football, and in some cases, both. He was recruited nationally for one sport or the other by nearly every major college sports program. Tim's first love was football; his second love was Amanda. The longer they dated, the more his second love shifted to become his first love.

Everyone in town and across the South was curious where Tim would go to college and play ball, but he took his time in making such an impactful decision. It wasn't until the middle of his senior year when Tim finally decided where he would begin his amazing journey. Tim made his college choice, and it wasn't what anyone had expected.

Tim chose Amanda. After all the recruiting trips, letters, coaches' visits, media attention, and constant pressure from friends and neighbors, Tim decided his love for Amanda outweighed what any college or sport could offer. It was far more important to him to stay in his hometown with Amanda than to go play college ball. He chose to marry his beautiful sweetheart and start a life together where they were raised and beloved.

Amanda tried to persuade Tim to go on to "bigger and better things" without her. Amanda would frequently attempt to encourage him to go to college, especially their senior year in high school. She would consistently say "Sports are your way out of this town. College can give you unlimited possibilities for your future. If you follow the college path that your amazing gifts as an athlete have provided you, your life can change forever."

She was exactly right, and he knew it. But those weren't the changes he was seeking. Tim knew neither he nor Amanda would be able to afford traveling back and forth to see one another, even if he chose the closest college available. He knew his life was forever transformed when he first asked Amanda to be his girlfriend in the eighth grade.

Amanda wanted to stay close to home so she could assist her elderly parents, who depended on her for their daily routine. Her parents had tried for years to have children but were unable to conceive for the first thirty-five years of their marriage. They had given up on the idea of having children and decided to turn their lives to solely serving the Lord, the church, and the community. They were completely surprised when they discovered they were pregnant with Amanda. As Amanda grew up, her parents spent a lot of time loving her, teaching her, supporting her, and preparing her for adulthood as best they could.

Amanda certainly could have gone to college. She had good enough grades to receive full scholarship offers to every school that also wanted Tim. With her parents in their poor health condition, she just couldn't allow herself to leave during that stage of her life. She was extremely smart and stunningly beautiful. More importantly, she was beautiful in character. Amanda was an unbelievable young woman. She was incredible in her faith in the Lord and in serving others, and she had an optimistic spirit that couldn't be shaken. Even with the multiple academic scholarship opportunities from across the country and a very likely financially successful career in her future, she felt called to serve her parents and her hometown.

Amanda's parents became very frail when she was in high school. Every morning and day after school, she did everything around the house for her parents. She did all the cooking, cleaning, yard work, and house repairs. She became very skilled at managing things adults usually handled. She wasn't getting the high school experience all her friends were getting, but she never complained. Tim spent a lot of his free time trying to help Amanda with some of the big chores, but she was a very proud young lady and never asked for help from anyone. She was a great athlete and a great student. She worked hard in sports, school, and life. Tim was constantly amazed by how well she managed all the different and difficult responsibilities in her life.

Amanda had to frequently answer questions about college by many well-intentioned people in town. Much of the stress that Amanda was feeling surfaced one day while Tim was helping her buy food and supplies at their local grocery store. A friendly lady from church, named Ann, approached the young couple, just as many others had in the past, to ask her some probing questions.

"Hey, hun. How are you doin' these days? I haven't seen you at any of the basketball games. You are still on the team, aren't you?" Ann asked.

"Hello, Ms. Ann. No, ma'am. I'm not on the team anymore." Amanda usually did her best to avoid talking about herself, especially about sports. With the stress of her parents' poor health, she no longer allowed sports to be an important part of her life.

"Well darlin', I don't understand why not. You're too good to not be playin'. You started every game in basketball and softball your entire high school career. It's your senior year. I noticed you didn't play softball this year either, but I thought for sure you would be playin' basketball. Did you do somethin' at school that caused them to not let you play?"

"No, ma'am. I did nothing wrong."

"Well I just don't get it. Why would anyone not play their senior year? This is the year you get scholarship offers. Believe me, everyone says you'd get 'em. In track alone, I read you were one of the fastest runners in the state. I know there've been a lot of people talkin' 'bout you not playin' sports this year and lettin' everyone down. I don't know anyone that knows why you're not playin'. You're eventually gonna have to come clean and tell someone. Are you sure nothin' happened? Do you want me to see if I can help get you back on the team?"

Tim had wandered a few isles over, looking for some chips before Ann arrived. As he rounded the corner, he was happily tossing his chips in the air and catching them. He only heard Amanda talking and had not heard any of what Ann had already said. Tim noticed that Amanda appeared to have tears in her eyes and was very animated as she spoke.

"Ms. Ann, nothing happened. Ok? I'm not trying to let everyone down. I don't *want* to let my teammates down. I don't *want* to let my school down. I'm sorry, but I don't have time to make everyone in this town happy. If I play sports, that takes *time*. It takes *time* to practice. It takes *time* to play games. It takes *time* to travel. I don't have extra time. I don't get to have sleepovers with my friends. I don't get to go to the dances. I don't get to go to parties. You know what I *get* to do? This. I *get* to go grocery shopping. I *get* to help Mom and Dad. I *get* to wash clothes and dishes. I *get* to clean the house, mow the yard, pay the bills, and stuff that is important."

Tim approached Ann and Amanda very cautiously. Both women looked at Tim and then stared at the floor. Nobody said a word. Amanda was embarrassed that she spoke out of frustration to Ms. Ann. Ms. Ann was embarrassed that she made so many assumptions about Amanda. Tim stood there for a moment and broke the awkward silence with the rattling of the bag of potato chips. When Amanda and Ann looked at Tim, he said, "And I *get* to help."

"Bless you, Tim. You're a good young man for helpin her with all this." Ann looked at Amanda and tried to make amends. "Amanda, sweetheart, I never even thought about how all this with your parents has impacted you. You have been such a blessin to your wonderful parents. Your momma and daddy have bragged to so many people about how much you have done and always do for them. I have been so rude. I know I couldn't have given up my senior year like you have and I wasn't even as smart or as good at sports as you are. Baby, I'm sorry. If there is anything me or my family can do to help you out, you just let me know."

"I'm sorry. Ms. Ann, I didn't mean to speak that way to you. I hope you will forgive me. You and everyone in town have been very helpful and my family is very grateful for everyone around here. Please excuse us, because we have to get back home now and put these groceries away."

Tim and Amanda paid for their stuff and loaded everything into the car. As they were driving home, Tim asked Amanda to pull over so they could discuss what had just happened.

After she pulled over and before he spoke, he turned his body so he could face her directly. He held her hand and calmly began to speak. "Amanda, I know all this has been hard on you. Everyone keeps asking you where you're going to college, why you're not playing sports, and other stuff that just isn't their business. I know you don't plan on leaving here. Other people don't know that, but I do. We keep talking about where we might go, but I know you don't want to leave.

"You keep trying to get me to go to college, but I want you to know, I'm not going anywhere. We talk all the time about the what ifs in our lives, but my what if is with you. You think you are holding me back, but you aren't. You make me better in every way. I hope you don't think I'm holding you back either. My heart belongs to you. My heart belongs in our hometown. Neither of us have been willing to say it, but I don't want to leave here. I don't think you want to either. I won't ever leave you. We have been going back and forth for the last few months talking about our plans, dreams, and aspirations. Baby, it has been fun to talk about all that, but the reality is, we *belong* here. We *belong* with each other. Our calling is to serve here. Our calling is to be together, forever. I love you very much, Amanda.

"I've been carrying this thing around for three weeks and was going to wait and do this during the perfect moment at the perfect spot. After what I just heard in there, I want to do this before you decide to skip town without me." Tim reached into his pocket and pulled out a crumpled matchbox. As he slid the matchbox open, he said, "I don't have a lot of money and I'm sorry this is all I could afford, but the good thing is, the insurance shouldn't cost much on it."

Amanda had tears in her eyes from his previous proclamation of love and when she saw him pull out the ring, she covered her face with her hands and began to cry harder.

"Don't cry." Tim looked at the ring again and tried cleaning it on his shirt to make it shine better. "It's not the most beautiful thing ever, but it's got character."

Amanda extended her finger so Tim could place the ring. "It's perfect. I love it. I love you."

"Is that a 'yes'?"

"Yes! Forever and ever. That's a yes."

After they graduated, Tim and Amanda were married at their local state park, and nearly everyone in town was there to watch these two hometown favorites tie the knot. It was a beautiful sunny day, and the park was packed. Amanda was breathtaking in her white wedding dress, and Tim was very handsome in his suit. They were the best looking and most promising pair in town.

Tim and Amanda were a great couple right from the start. Unfortunately, not everyone saw it that way. In the small southern town, it was an unfamiliar sight to see a young black boy with a man-sized body dating a pretty, young white girl. Even as well liked as Tim was, he was still black, and she was still white. Everyone loved Tim, but not everyone loved the idea of Tim dating a white girl. Many of the people in town enjoyed seeing the two youngsters so happy together, but it took other people much longer before they became comfortable with the idea of them spending so much time together. Eventually, his character outweighed his color, even to the old-timers who hung on to beliefs that had been passed down from generations of ignorance.

Those in support of Tim and Amanda's relationship claimed they were the couple with a "match made in heaven, by the Lord Himself." People were right. Everyone loved them, and they were great for each other, to each other, to their parents, and to their community. Tim and Amanda were such great people; the people of the town adored them. Amanda's parents died shortly after she and Tim married, and everyone expected them to go on to college at that point, but they were happy serving their hometown.

Tim had lost his parents in a car accident during his junior year in high school, and this loss brought him and Amanda even closer. Tim's brother, Mike, was five years older than his little brother, so when their parents died, Tim moved in with Mike, and they toughed it out together.

Mike never left his hometown. He was a hardworking country boy. He liked to hunt, fish, and play ball. He wasn't quite the athlete Tim was, but when he was still in high school, he was the best athlete around. After he graduated high school, he went to the local junior college for two years and further developed his skills to become a mechanic. He always enjoyed working with his hands and didn't particularly enjoy school. He went to the junior college not to play ball but because he knew that, with the certifications he could receive there, he would eventually be able to make more money. He worked a full-time job the whole time he was in school, so he didn't spend any time out partying or goofing around like a lot of the other students. He worked, studied, and tried to be a leader and great example to his little brother.

Mike had a small apartment near the garage where he worked, and he really stepped up when their parents died. He willingly and selflessly took on the role of big brother and father figure to Tim. Tim was very grateful for his brother's sacrifice, but there were certainly times he didn't want Mike telling him what to do.

Both Mike and Amanda pushed Tim in school and in sports. Tim loved to play ball, but he also wanted to help Amanda more and more with her parents. Mike consistently fussed on Tim for not putting enough effort into his school and sports commitments, and Tim didn't appreciate the rebuke from his big brother. He didn't seem to mind it as much when Amanda said the same things to him. Both Amanda and Mike knew that Tim could be a superior college athlete if he pushed himself, but he spent every spare moment around her.

Everyone felt the passing of Tim's parents killed his spirit to play college ball, but really it was his love for Amanda that surpassed his incredible passion for sports. Their small town embraced and seemed to unofficially adopt the young, married, orphaned couple. Everyone loved them and did what they could to help them succeed. No one ever even heard whispers of things like "waste of talent" or "it's a shame they didn't go to college." From the moment they announced they weren't leaving for college, it just seemed right. Nobody ever questioned them or criticized their decision. In fact, the whole town seemed to quietly celebrate getting to keep such treasures for themselves.

These two lovebirds were mature beyond their youthful years. Tim became a full-time maintenance worker at the local state park where he and Amanda got married. In his every spare moment, he helped coach the young boys and girls at the middle school. His love for sports went from playing to coaching and mentoring. He was known as "Coach D," because all Tim's buddies called him "Dozer," short for "Bulldozer." Tim was a big, strong man. To the kids, he appeared to be a superhero. He stood at six three and weighed 220 pounds, with very little body fat. He looked like a grown man who could bench-press a truck.

All the children in town looked up to him, because of the way he treated, played, and interreacted with them. Because of Tim's personality and looks; all the mothers in town were enthralled with him too, and they seemed to have perfect attendance when he requested their presence at practices. All the kids had heard stories from their parents about when Tim played high school sports, and they always asked him to tell the stories to them. The hard work at the state park made him appear a lot older than he actually was, but he was still impressive in his stature. He was the most gentle and generous creature God had ever made and would do anything for anybody. Tim was the funniest person Amanda had ever known, and he could always make her laugh. One of his greatest gifts was that he knew exactly how to hold her when she cried.

Amanda served their town in many capacities. Through her ailing parents, she became very well known at the local hospital for her sensitive nature and her strong work ethic. She was always there and was always willing to help others. She wasn't a nurse, but everyone treated her like she was part of the staff. She eventually got hired full-time to assist patients with their recovery in a nonmedical way. She sat and interacted with patients and/or their families. Depending on what was needed at the time, she would either sit quietly, read, pray, or cry. She always seemed to know exactly what to do for each occasion.

Amanda had a healing spirit about her. She seemed to make people feel better just by being in the room. The hospital administrators knew she was incredibly smart and was blessed with a gift of healing. According to many patients, she was "an angel of the Lord." Nobody could really explain it, but people were just better while around her. Her presence seemed to be all the medicine and therapy some patients needed. Others wanted her to be around because they felt it would make their passing more comfortable when their time was imminent.

Tim knew exactly what it was; he claimed Amanda had a direct line to Jesus. He had never seen anyone pray as much as her or seem to truly enjoy a relationship with Jesus the way she did. He joked with her all the time that he was such a mess that God had sent a real-life angel to marry him and keep him straight.

Amanda loved not only the hospital but also her church. She spent a lot of her time cleaning the church and helping elderly people who were unable to attend services. She and Tim also taught a children's Sunday school class together. Most of the time, while teaching the class, Amanda felt like Tim was just another one of the kids. Tim was great with children, because he was still a kid himself.

When Jaxon was born, the whole town seemed to show up and support the Bulls. Jaxon was their first child and instantly seemed to be the "first son" of the small Mississippi town. As it turned out, Jaxon was their only child. They thought they would have several children, but that wasn't the Lord's plan for them. To Amanda, one kid was probably enough considering how much Jaxon got hurt and how often she had to keep her eyes glued to him and Tim.

To hear Amanda tell the story of Jaxon's first trip to the hospital as a patient, it was "because of Tim." Jaxon seemed to skip learning to walk and went straight to flying. Even at an early age, it was obvious that Jaxon had inherited his parents' intelligence and athletic abilities. According to Tim, it was only to "develop Jaxon's coordination" that he and Jaxon wrestled on the living room floor as part of their daily routine.

Once on a regular Saturday afternoon, Tim had just gotten home from work and was being rambunctious with Jaxon, just like usual. Their babysitter was a sweet high school girl named Cissy; she was gathering her belongings so she could leave the two rowdy boys on their own to play.

Normally, Cissy had Jaxon all to herself on a Saturday while both parents were at work. But on this particular day, Tim decided to come home early and couldn't wait to play with his "mini me." Cissy always claimed that she had a perfect record of Jaxon not getting hurt as long as Tim wasn't around. She jokingly said that under her supervision, Jaxon never got hurt until Tim came along and messed things up.

Cissy was the daughter of the small-town pastor and his wife, who lived next door to the Bulls. The pastor and his wife were a couple who loved the Lord and helping young people. They often treated Tim and Amanda like they were their own kids. Tim and Amanda moved into the small, two-bedroom house, owned by the church, because it was affordable, and it allowed them to live in the middle of town. It made routine things, such as going to church, getting groceries, and helping at the school, more convenient for the young, financially challenged couple.

A lot of people in the Bulls' life credited Jaxon's toughness on the field to the roughhouse style of play between Jaxon and Tim. Amanda was always a nervous wreck when they played, because she said it was like a small child and a large child imitating superheroes, and someone or something was bound to get broken. Jaxon was dangerously trusting and unquestionably fearless.

Most of Jaxon's visits to the hospital were social calls, and Cissy and Tim were the first ones that took him for a reason that wasn't. Amanda was at the hospital that Saturday, working in the emergency room, when she got word that her husband and son were there. She was excited about the surprise visit from her two loves, but as she walked into the waiting room, she quickly realized it wasn't a social visit. Jaxon was smiling ear to ear with red stains on his face, hands, and shirt. Tim had the look of a child about to get scolded by his mother.

"He's okay!" Tim said to his bride as he threw his hands up in a defensive position. "Before you go crazy, know he's fine."

Cissy stood behind Tim and Jaxon with her hands in the air. "Not my fault, Amanda."

The ironic thing was it was only days after Jaxon had been first knocked out in the living room floor. Because she never realized Jaxon was unconscious that day, Tim and Jaxon avoided getting in trouble with Amanda. They weren't as fortunate this time around. You would think after dodging such a bullet with Amanda, they would have been more careful, at least for a while. Adventure and common sense rarely lined up when those two were playing together.

Jaxon was habitually playing with his dad and jumping off everything in sight. Tim always tried to be safe with Jaxon, but his own adventurous spirit often took over and became intertwined with Jaxon's. Jaxon had been playing on the floor with Cissy, but now that Tim was home, he'd decided to climb on the couch and make a leap to the coffee table. The table, like everything else they had, was neither new nor very attractive. It was used and abused furniture someone had given them. Most of what they had were hand-me-downs, but Tim and Amanda did a great job of making everything look perfect. Tim moved the old coffee table out of the way for them to have more playing room, and Jaxon didn't realize it was too far away for him to land the jump. In his mind, he could make it no matter where it was in the house.

Tim gently slid the table over, then quickly got up and went to the next room. He was getting his money together to pay Cissy and say goodbye. While he and Cissy were in the other room, they heard a loud bang, but there was no burst of crying. They could still hear Jaxon making noise, so they didn't think Jaxon was injured. They both assumed he probably had thrown something.

Tim's first thought was, *Oh, no! Amanda is going to kill us if we break something else.* He and Cissy slowly poked their heads around the corner and saw Jaxon trying to shove the coffee table closer to the couch. Jaxon was wearing his comfortable, ragged denim overalls with a white T-shirt on underneath. His head was down, his arms extended, and he was pushing with all his might against the old, heavy table, but it wasn't moving an inch. His feet slid on the floor as he pushed against the seemingly immovable object. Because his feet were moving, he felt like he was making some real progress. He wasn't going to jump short this time.

Because he was on a mission, Jaxon hadn't noticed his own blood yet. Tim calmly walked over, and as he towered over his young son, he asked, "What are you doing there, little Bulldozer?"

When Jaxon looked up, that's when Tim saw the cut and the blood. He knew right away that Jaxon was going to need stitches; more importantly, Amanda was going to ground both of them from their high-flying act for a while. He glanced over at Cissy and said, "I haven't paid you yet. You're still on the clock. You're going with us! Amanda won't kill me with you standing there." He paused for a moment and jokingly said, "Besides, I'm blaming you for this whole mess!"

Jaxon never cried. Not once. Not a single tear. Tim knew very early on that his kid was as tough as nails. This was beyond what he expected though. This was different. This would have made any kid cry. Something about this kid was different from all the kids he had ever worked with before. Any one of the kids in the junior high group he worked with would have cried in response to this cut or the sight of his or her own blood.

Even after working in the hospital all this time, Amanda still didn't like the sight of blood. The hospital wasn't much of a hospital, and the emergency room was more similar to a waiting room at most rural doctor's offices. They lived in such a small town that the term *hospital* was used loosely. Nevertheless, it served most of the needs of normal household accidents and routine visits. The thought of her baby bleeding wasn't something she was too excited about.

The sight of blood on her son was unbearable to the young, nervous mother. Even though Tim calmly said, "He's okay," Amanda quickly grabbed her son but couldn't look at his injury. They were at the hospital for what seemed like only a matter of minutes, and everyone there already knew about the need for Jaxon's first stitches.

Jaxon was always a favorite at the hospital. Just like his mother, people seemed to feel better when he was around. Even at a very young age, he had an instinct for making people happy and feel good. All the nurses wanted to come by and see him and his battle scar. His mother wasn't so happy about the reason for the attention and wasn't going to let that fear ever leave her in life. This was her baby, and she was terrified by the thought of him ever getting hurt. Tim, on the other hand, was high-fiving his son as the stitches were getting put in his tiny, little chin.

# 3
## Lessons of Identity

Jaxon, still lying on his back, can now see, but still he cannot hear anything except his heart violently beating within.

He can see bright, white light. It is unbearably bright! That is really all he can see, but at least it is not dark anymore. Still not speaking, Jaxon wonders where all the bright light is coming from. He begins to blink, and he holds his eyes tightly closed to try to get some relief from the bright light.

As he continues to hold his eyes shut and slowly open them back up, he notices the light change from white to yellow, to green, and to red. That isn't the change he is hoping for, but at least it was a change. As the light changed from solid white to a variety of colors, he thinks back to a childhood conversation with his dad after a confusing day of playing with his friends.

Tim was in front of the house one beautiful Saturday afternoon, working on the family car. He had the hood open, and he leaned halfway into the motor. All Jaxon could see were his dad's legs and part of his torso. Tim wore his "lucky work jeans," which looked like he had been wearing them while painting every house in town and working on half the cars and trucks in the county. Jaxon could hear a wrench turning and his dad grunting. He was trying his best not to bother Tim, because he knew he was busy, but the mind of a child never stops working just because his dad is wrapped up in something else.

Unfortunately, Tim had to spend a lot of time working on the family car. Tim and Amanda had bought the car from Mike for practically nothing. Someone had taken it to the car shop where Mike worked, and after he got it running again, he informed the owner of the price for the repairs, and the owner told him to keep the car. He claimed the car wasn't worth what it had taken Mike to do the repairs. When Mike told Tim about the car, he told him it would take a little elbow grease to keep it running but that he could have it for the price of the repairs.

"Daddy, what am I?" Jaxon asked in a low and slightly confused voice.

Tim momentarily stopped turning his wrench, not sure whether he had heard his son. After pausing for a moment and not hearing anything else, he hesitantly asked, "Excuse me?" Tim cautiously waited for a response to see whether someone was actually there.

"What am I?" Jaxon asked again.

Tim wore a backward, greasy "Angels Football" ball cap. He slightly raised his head, turned to glance over his shoulder, and asked, "Did you just say, 'What am I?'"

"Yes, sir,"

"I'll tell you what you're not. That's a mechanic. If you were, I'd have your little butt up here fixing this car."

Jaxon just stood there patiently with a blank expression on his face, respectfully waiting on the answer.

Tim wasn't sure if his son was joking and then realized it was a serious question. "What do you mean, 'What am I?' I don't know what you mean," Tim then stood all the way up, leaned against the car, grabbed his grease rag, and started wiping his hands.

Jaxon looked at him, intently. "I mean, what color am I?"

Tim stopped wiping his hands and slowly walked toward his son. While still holding his rag and shifting it from one hand to the other to give himself time to contemplate a response, he stared down at Jaxon. "That's an interesting question you've got there. Why do you ask?"

"We were playing football in Mark's backyard when Joey called me 'black,' but Mark said I was 'white.'"

Tim straightened his posture, leaned his head back, and slightly giggled. "Why were they calling you colors?"

"We were playing football, but there was only three of us, so I said I would be the all-time quarterback. Joey said I couldn't be the quarterback, because his daddy said black quarterbacks only ran the ball, and he wanted me to throw the ball. Then he said that his daddy said I was a black boy. Mark said I wasn't a black boy, that I was a white boy. They both started arguing, and then they asked me what I was."

Tim laughed to himself about his son's realization that he really had no concept of what color he was. "What'd you tell 'em?"

"I told them, 'I'm a quarterback!' and then I told Joey to 'go deep,'" Jaxon said with full confidence while holding the ball up to show his dad.

Tim started laughing at Jaxon's response. "That a boy! You be the quarterback if you wanna be the quarterback. Don't let nobody tell you otherwise."

"But daddy, what color am I?"

Tim squatted down and got face-to-face with Jaxon so he could look him in the eyes. "Son, you think your momma gave birth to a crayon?"

Jaxon appeared extremely confused by his dad's question. "Huh?"

"You heard me. Do you think your momma gave birth to a crayon?"

"No, sir," Jaxon appeared extremely confused by the question.

"Jax, you ain't no crayon. You ain't no color. You're not black, and you're not white. You're a Bull. You are my son, and your momma's son."

"But Daddy—" Jaxon started to ask a question before Tim interrupted him.

"Son, let me finish. Jax, you remember in our Bible story the other night that little David was called 'a man after God's own heart'?"

"Yes, sir,"

"Son, that's what you are. You are a man after God's own heart. Right now, you're just a little boy after mine and your momma's own heart, but one day that will change. When you get old enough to develop your own relationship with the Lord, everything will change for you. You will pursue God, just like King David did."

Jaxon defended himself. "Daddy, I do have a relationship with Jesus."

Tim, trying to reassure his son, said, "I know you do, Jax. But one day it will be different. One day you'll understand it better, and you'll know what I mean. You understand, Son?"

Jaxon, staring at Tim, nodded, "But what do I tell people who ask if I am black or white?"

"Son, colors don't matter. If someone is ever trying to get you to claim to be a certain color, first of all, that is somebody who needs Jesus. I would also be curious to know why your color even mattered to them."

"But I thought everyone needed Jesus."

"You're right, Son. *Everyone* needs Jesus. When you interact with people, your first priority in life should be to make sure they know His love beyond colors and everything else. If someone asks you what color you are, you tell them you're 'the color of Jesus's love.' If they ask you what color that is, you tell them to 'ask Him.' It's not a color that makes a man. It's his heart and how he treats others that make a man.

If you love God with all your heart and treat everyone the way Jesus would, your color will be the least important subject. I don't want you thinking about yourself in terms of color. I don't want you to ever worry about the color of someone else either. You treat everyone with respect and love them like Jesus would. You make certain that when people see you, they don't see a color. They see Jesus's love."

"You mean the way you and Momma love each other?"

"Similar to that but way better. You'll be better than all of us, Son, because you have some of me and your momma in you but mostly because you have Jesus in you. And that is the most important thing."

Jaxon started smiling as Tim continued. "I will go ahead and tell you now, Son, but you will also learn this on your own in life. As you get older, you will have opportunities to do nothing, to do something small, to do something great, or to do something everlasting. You will be able to make choices that can affect yourself and choices that will affect others. Those decisions may impact only that particular moment or may affect the future. You will also be able to make decisions that can impact eternity. Those decisions will determine what type of label the world will try to put on you. If you make great decisions, black folks and white folks will try to label you as one of their own. If you mess up, both will deny you. Everyone will claim you are the opposite as them. They will claim the reason you messed up is because you have something in you that isn't what they are."

Jaxon started to appear a little confused and a little bored. He shifted from one foot to the other but still paid attention to his father. Tim said, "You're gonna have to work extra hard to determine who you are in this life, because others are sure gonna try to do it for you. Others will try to put you in a box they can mark on a form. Don't just label yourself as a race but as a child of God. Labels are for folks too lazy to get to know someone for themselves. Those kinds of folks rely too much on preconceived ideas of who people are. Labels are also for people so lazy they just lean on their friend's or family's reputation or history instead of working hard to earn their own good name. People think labels will make it easier to determine how they are supposed to treat someone else, how they are supposed to act themselves, or how others will treat them. Choosing the wrong label can make us appear to be victims when in reality we are all victims if we rely on a label to represent us instead of our relationships with one another. What a person looks like or where they come from should have no bearing on how we treat others or how the world treats us.

"Your mom and I wouldn't and still won't allow our relationship with one another to be defined by something neither of us had anything to do with. She didn't pick being white, and I didn't pick being black. We didn't pick our parents; nor did our parents pick us. What you are in life should be determined by what you do and how you do it more than just being born. With God's prompting, your mom picked me, and I picked her. By the grace of God, we built what we have on our hard work and our love for one another. In this life, you will get what you put into it. If you go around blaming life and others for your problems, you will only experience problems. How hard you work, how you treat others, how you respond to this world, and how you represent and follow Jesus—those are the things that will matter to others more than any worldly label. If everyone claims you are one of them, you are probably on the right track. If everyone is denying you are one of them, you better start pokin' your nose in the mirror. Son, what I'm saying is, don't label yourself with the options the world provides you. God already labeled you before you were even born when He called you 'mine.' You just make sure to always remember that and to live your life in a way that will not dishonor that label."

Tim, feeling great about his speech, asked, "Do you think you're ready to answer your friends now when they ask you what you are?"

"Yes, sir."

"Good. Well, what are you going to tell them?"

Jaxon looked up and smiled. "If they ask me again, I'm going to tell them to ask *you*."

Tim laughed at his son, then spread his fingers wide and ran his greasy hand down Jaxon's face. Three of his fingers left oily stripes. Tim said, "I'll tell you what you are. You're a zebra! Now go play so I can get this car back in shape."

# 4
## Speak Up

Jaxon is beginning to be able to make out an image standing over him. The bright colors are fading, and there is a blurry figure starting to take form before his eyes. He can't quite tell what it is, but he is happy that he no longer feels like there is a spotlight pointing directly at his face.

He can now make out his friend and teammate, Phoenix, towering over him. Phoenix appears to be saying something. Jaxon sees Phoenix's mouth moving but cannot understand what he is saying. Phoenix shouts louder and louder. *"Bull!* Are you okay, Bull? Bull! Wake up, Bull! Get up!"

Phoenix frantically waves at the sidelines for the trainers to come out to his fallen teammate. Phoenix can't believe it. The Bull always gets up. The Bull is the guy who puts others on their backs; he shouldn't be on his back. Phoenix is extremely worried about his motionless friend.

Andy Fisher was the first trainer onto the field. He is only a student trainer, but because he is a senior, he is the most veteran of all the student trainers, and he is allowed to assist in most of the on-field injuries. He sprints past the professional athletic trainers, players, and coaches as if he were an Olympic gold medal winner. He shouts along the way, "Back away from him! Don't touch him! Get back!" The concerned crowd of players standing around their fallen teammate begin to slowly back away.

As he approaches his injured friend's head, Andy slides to his knees and gets into the proper position for a suspected head or neck injury. With his knees pointed toward Jaxon's shoulders and bent at the waist, he firmly holds Jaxon's head completely stable, with one hand on either side of his helmet. By this point, Jaxon has closed his eyes again. Andy begins shouting, "Wake up! Wake up, Jax! J, can you hear me?"

He can see Jaxon is breathing but he's not responding to his shouts. Andy raises his head to see who else is near and shouts, "Hurry up!" The other trainers all arrive shortly after Andy and begin going through the proper protocols. Because the trainers are so fast to the scene, there are still several players in the area. One trainer starts clearing the other players away from their injured brother, and another trainer begins checking for any signs of bleeding or visible injuries without moving Jaxon. Many of the offensive players and several of the defensive players haven't yet even realized Jaxon is hurt.

Jaxon understands something is terribly wrong, but he has an unbelievable calm about him while everyone around him is scrambling and worrying. As his vision is slowly restoring, he knows he isn't blind, but he begins to wonder whether he is now deaf. He can make out images but still not hear anything. Laying on the cold, hard ground, he can smell all the familiar smells of football in the air: the sweat of other players, the perfectly manicured grass, and a slight hint of popcorn and bourbon in the air. He is able to maintain a slight sense of optimism and humor as he thought, *Well, at least I can smell.*

He is still trying to figure out what is wrong. He continues staring at Andy's mouth, desperately trying to understand what he is saying. Jaxon anxiously tries to communicate with his friend, but so far, he is completely unsuccessful. He believes he is telling Andy to "speak up and stop mumbling," but not even the slightest sound is coming from his mouth.

"Speak up, Son. Don't mumble. Speak clearly. Let the world know you're there." That was the advice Tim gave his five-year-old son out in the yard after he asked Jaxon what had happened. Tim told Jaxon to wait for him, because he needed to run into the house to get his glove and said he would be right back. When he got inside their house, he heard the sound of breaking glass, followed by a scattered crash. Tim knew right away that Jaxon had thrown the ball into the window but chose to ask his nervous son about the incident.

"Hey, Jax! Come here, Son" were the words Jaxon dreaded to hear as his father came strolling back into the yard. Jaxon dropped his head and walked toward his father at a snail's pace. He was making no record time crossing the yard and wouldn't dare look at his father.

"What was that sound I just heard, Son?" Tim asked.

"I don't know," Jaxon said to his father as he kept his eyes on the ground.

Tim dropped down to one knee. "Son, do you know I love you?"

"Yes, sir."

With his large hand on his tiny son's shoulder, Tim asked, "Do you believe me if I tell you I will love you know matter what?"

Jaxon kept his eyes out of sight and his voice at a barely audible level. "Yes, sir."

With one hand still on Jaxon's shoulder, Tim reached out with his other hand and touched the bottom of his son's chin. "Son, lift your head and look me in the eye when you speak. Do you understand me?"

Jaxon slightly raised his chin with a little bit of help from his father. He was standing in the small amount of grass in the Bulls' tiny front yard and looked his father directly in the eyes. Tim again reassured his son, "Jax, you are my son, and I will always love you. You need to know that. You also need to know that you can trust me, and you should never lie. It is really hard to trust a man after he has lied to you, and I never want to doubt anything you tell me. Are you following me?"

Jaxon shook his head indicating he understood. "You're not a puppet, Son. You can speak. When you speak, speak as if you have something to say. Do not be afraid to ever give me your answer, no matter how bad you think it is. The truth is always worth saying out loud."

"Yes, sir," Jaxon cautiously said to his father.

Tim pointed in the direction of where the sound had come from, knowing full well what had happened. "All right, Son, I want to know. Do you know what that sound was?"

This time Jaxon gave a slightly more confident but somewhat hesitant answer. "Yes, sir."

"Well, what was that sound?"

Jaxon glanced toward the broken window and pointed his tiny index finger. "I threw the ball."

While still down on his knees, facing his son, Tim said, "That ball sure made a weird sound when you threw it. You ever heard one make that kind of sound before?"

"No, sir."

"You know, I remember hearing one make that sound before. I believe I was about your age when I threw a ball that made that very same racket. I also remember my dad asking me what that noise was, and I knew what it was, but I didn't want to tell him, because I was afraid he would be mad at me. You know what he told me?"

Jaxon looked up at his father and with a slightly curious tone in his voice asked, "What?"

"He stared directly at me, just like I am looking at you. He said, 'Son, if you did something on accident, I will not be upset with you if you are honest with me about it. We will do our best to fix it, learn from it, and try to do better next time. Then we will both get on down the road. What will disappoint me, though, is if you do not trust me enough to tell me the truth. I trust you enough to tell you the truth, and I always want you to do the same for me.' Son, every time I, or anyone else, ever asks you a question, you will have two options to choose from. You will choose to be honest or dishonest. In the moment, the choice may seem difficult, and I will not try to convince you it will always feel like an easy choice. Your character will be built on the hard choices you make. Your life will be defined by the hard choices you make. Are you up for making the right choice, even if it is a hard one?"

Jaxon was starting to realize what his father was getting at. "Yes, sir."

"Well, Son, can you tell me what happened?"

Now prepared to answer thoroughly, Jaxon pointed at the window. "I broke the window. It broke when I threw the ball. I didn't mean to."

Tim smiled at his son. "I am very proud of you for telling me the truth. I am glad that you didn't get hurt. You are not in trouble, J. Accidents have always happened, and they always will. When we throw the ball, though, we always need to be careful where we throw it and not throw toward things that will break. When we break things, we have to replace them. If we have to replace things, we can't afford more balls to throw. Now, do you want to tell your momma, or do you want me to?"

Jaxon started to chuckle and shook his head. "You, Daddy."

"That's what I was afraid you'd say." He started playfully shaking his fist toward Jaxon and jokingly said, "You know she's going to make you get a job, don't you?"

Jaxon started laughing and said, "Daddy!"

Tim picked up his son, stood to his feet, and gave him a big hug. They walked back inside the house to retrieve the ball.

# 5
# Fishing for Friends

Andy continues yelling into Jaxon's face, "Can you hear me? Bull, are you okay? Can you hear me?" Jaxon has a slight, barely noticeable smile come across his face.

Jaxon's eyes shift from Andy's eyes to his mouth as he tries his best to understand what his longtime friend is saying. As he continues lying on the ground, he notices seemingly muffled sounds. He can hear what sounds like people talking as if they are off in the distance.

Jaxon always made friends easily. At a young age, he made friends with those around him everywhere he went. Everyone instantly liked him and constantly wanted to be around him. Well, nearly everyone liked him instantly. It took a little encouragement for Andy Fisher to like him.

It was the first day of class in the third grade of Andy's new school when Jaxon became friends with Andy Fisher. Andy had recently moved to the small town and had yet to make any friends. He spotted Jaxon in class but thought he had failed a grade because he was so much larger than everyone else.

Andy was small and weak. He was intimidated by Jaxon's size, even from a distance. The only person he had met at school so far was the teacher. Andy was a shy kid who was happy to leave his last school but not excited about being at a new one. He always had trouble making friends. In fact, he didn't have any friends. At his last school he had gotten picked on a lot, and he really disliked going. He was always skeptical of other children, because he was easily targeted. He was repeatedly the one to get made fun of or picked on. Being small and weak, he was also sick a lot as a kid. He didn't enjoy going to school any more than he enjoyed going to the dentist. He was certain this school was going to be no different. Why would these kids treat him any differently than every kid he had ever met before?

The first time any of the students ever laid eyes on Andy was that morning just before going out to the playground. The teacher had been giving the class lesson when she heard a knock on the classroom door. She politely asked the class to excuse her as she went to see who it was. The principal had a frail, young student with her and said, "This here is Andy Fisher. He and his family are brand new to our school, and he is now in your class. Y'all take good care of him."

The teacher put her hands on her hips, dropped her head, and cautiously gazed down at the new student. She smiled at Andy and said, "Well, I guess we can handle one more." She opened the door farther and allowed him into her classroom. She joyfully said to the class, "Boys and girls, this is Andy. He will be your new classmate. We are in the middle of this lesson, so when we finish, we are going to recess. When we go outside, you can talk to him then. Let's finish up before we start talking and making him feel welcome."

With that she directed Andy to his seat while the others looked at him as if he were an unknown species. From the time the teacher opened the door till he sat down at his desk, Andy never took his eyes off the floor.

By the time the teacher's lesson was over, the kids were so excited to go to the playground that they had completely forgotten about Andy. They were far more interested in recess with their friends than in meeting a stranger. When the bell rang, they all quickly lined up at the door. Andy was the last one in line as the class exited into the hallway. The teacher led them all down the hallway, and they were revved up like stock cars getting ready to run the Daytona 500. When the teacher opened the door leading to the playground, they were off to the races. Andy was unfamiliar with the layout of the playground, so he slowly walked out and cautiously observed the environment.

After about twenty minutes, Andy decided he didn't want to sit on the sidelines any longer. He saw a group of boys climbing on the jungle gym and figured that if he climbed to the top and stood up, he would impress them enough that he would go from being invisible to instantly being the king of the third grade.

Just moments before, Jaxon had already proved he held the throne for the third-grade class as the king of the playground. His athleticism allowed him to be prominent in any group. There was a large crowd on the playground that day when Jaxon stepped into the middle of it to make his presence known. An older kid on the playground was calling him out for one of the many schoolyard challenges he faced.

Jaxon was younger, but he wasn't small or weak. He was a man among boys throughout all his school days. He was smaller than the older kid, but that didn't intimidate or scare him. He never really had to develop into his athleticism. Most kids his size and at his age were clumsy and awkward. Jaxon always excelled athletically. There were lots of older kids who knew of Jaxon from Little League, and they knew how physically gifted he was. Older kids frequently challenged him at school or baseball games. He didn't always win, but he held his own and grew more confident with each challenge he faced.

Jaxon's classmates were chanting, "Ja-xon! Ja-xon! Ja-xon" as he slowly approached the group. Jaxon stepped into the circle, where he appeared cocky and proud to represent all third-graders across the entire world. This was his moment. He was here for triumph!

Jaxon was the tallest one in his class, and he loved the attention. He was one who didn't go out of his way to seek attention, but when the spotlight was on him, he soaked it up with great enthusiasm. His challenger that day was the fourth-grade's playground champion. He had already beaten all the kids in his class several times throughout the year. As he searched for a bold enough challenger, one of Jaxon's fellow third-graders shouted out with great pride, "Jaxon can beat you!"

The unimpressed fourth-grader looked around and laughed. He wasn't worried. This wasn't the first time this had happened. This proud third-grader was once again defending his athletic abilities and his class. The fourth-grade champ had beaten Jaxon on several other occasions, but each time Jaxon stepped up to the challenge as if he knew he was going to win each time. He had bold confidence no matter what the challenge was or how many times he had been defeated. His confidence never failed him.

All the kids lined up on the playground, with each class representing their champion. Jaxon was on one side and the fourth-grade racing master on the other. There were two kids waiting at the far end of the playground with arms bound together to create a makeshift finish line. Jaxon stepped to the starting line. The official starting line was created by a kid who dragged his foot in the dirt and boldly announced, "To your mark!"

All the kids counted together, "One! Two! Three! ... Go!"

Jaxon shot out of there like a bullet. He knew today was going to be different. He felt faster. He felt stronger. The fourth-grader also knew right away that he was going to have to run harder today than he had ever run against Jaxon before. He knew today that Jaxon was a worthy challenger to his title as "the fastest kid on the playground."

Jaxon took an early lead, and a cocky smile came across his face. The entire third-grade class erupted with excitement. Even Andy, sitting from a distance, found himself clapping and cheering for this stranger he was certain would only eventually bring him pain.

The fourth-grader then found an extra gear and took the lead halfway down the playground's imaginary track. The third-graders became nervous as the fourth-grade side began cheering and laughing. They laughed because they knew their champion would win, as he always had in the past.

Jaxon quickly lost his boastful smile as he briefly began to trail. He took the lead once again, only to lose it just as they crossed the tiny human finish line.

After all the excitement and commotion died down, everyone slowly returned to the swing sets, jungle gyms, and other random pieces of playground equipment. Nobody seemed too upset, because Jaxon always lost to the fourth grade's champion. He could beat a few others in the classes above him, but he could never beat another class's champion.

He lost the race that day but knew something was different. He knew that was the closest he had ever come to beating the fastest kid on the playground. The fourth-grader knew it too. He knew that race had been way too close, and he almost lost his title to a third-grader. That would be an insufferable embarrassment. He would never race Jaxon on the playground again.

Jaxon lost the race that day, but he had also won. He gained a psychological advantage that would help him the rest of his playing days. It only fueled his desire to compete against the best. He didn't seek to compete against those he didn't feel were a challenge to him.

He wanted to beat the best. Easy wins weren't what he desired. He was hungry for serious challenges.

Andy sat on the highest point of the playground and carefully watched as all this unfolded. He didn't know any of these kids, but he couldn't help noticing that Jaxon seemed to be the most popular person he had ever laid eyes on. He automatically disliked and feared him. He knew Jaxon was just like all the other bullies in his life. He knew that as soon as Jaxon finished the race, he would find him like a heat-seeking missile just so he could ridicule the new kid. He already began to dislike him, even though he hadn't yet met him.

He sat in the grass under an old, large shade tree, where a few of the teachers were trying to escape the unbearable, southern heat. He sat with his legs crossed, wearing his favorite blue jeans and a nice collared shirt, just plucking away at the clovers as he observed the race of the century. He remained secluded in the safety of the shade until after the race. After everyone dispersed from the competition, he spotted a group of boys on the lower rungs of the playground's jungle gym. He stood up and stared intently for a few moments as he formulated his plan to become the new playground hero.

He deliberately walked down the hill toward the imposing jungle gym. His heart started beating faster and faster with each step in anticipation of the challenge ahead. There were no kids higher than the halfway point of the jungle gym, and there were surely none *brave* enough to stand on top of the playground's centerpiece. There were about five or six other boys, including Jaxon, already on the jungle gym as Andy grabbed the first bar. He paused for a moment, reached up, and slowly began to ascend the mountain of worn, painted metal.

As he climbed, the other boys stopped talking and carefully watched him with great curiosity. Andy cautiously climbed and looked only toward the top of the jungle gym, not making eye contact with any of his new classmates. Once he reached the summit, he made his conquering move. He sat down, got his feet meticulously into position, and carefully leaned forward, grabbing the bars at his feet. Once he began to stand, the other boys watched him like he was crazy. As he extended his legs, he had to let go of the bars to stand fully erect.

Everything was going according to plan until he looked up. Upon looking victoriously toward the sky, he lost his balance and fell. He went straight through the bars and hit the solid ground below. They could hear the loud thud of his frail frame slamming into the ground, followed by every bit of oxygen in his body being violently forced out.

The other kids weren't above the halfway point of the jungle gym because they weren't allowed. It wasn't because they were scared, as Andy had suspected. The young boys knew that once Andy reached the peak, he would be immediately spotted by the teachers under the shade tree, and he would never set foot on the playground again. It would be, at best, playground solitary confinement or, at worst, a playground privileges death sentence. When Andy fell, all the other kids scattered to avoid being incriminated with this new hooligan.

Andy was hurt and unable to get up and run with the others. He had hit the ground tremendously hard, and nobody wanted to get near him, fearful of getting in trouble. Jaxon noticed right away that the new kid wasn't moving and chose to go and offer his assistance. He cautiously approached his fallen classmate and realized Andy's eyes were closed and he was moaning in pain.

When Andy finally opened his eyes, Jaxon was leaning over him, smiling, and staring directly into his eyes. He emphatically said, "Hi, I'm Jaxon."

Andy closed his eyes and struggled to regain his breath. When he reopened his eyes, Jaxon was still there. Jaxon had gotten on his knees and was bent at the waist, where he could better see Andy's face. "Hey there. You all right? I'm Jaxon. Boy, I sure bet that hurt!"

Andy couldn't make out what he was saying, because he was still disoriented, so he just kept looking at Jaxon. Jaxon repeated himself, "Are you okay? Andy, can you hear me?"

Andy, extremely embarrassed and in pain, struggled to say, "How do you know my name?"

"You're Andy. Our teacher told us. Don't you remember? Let me help you." Jaxon helped Andy sit up, and after a few moments for Andy to regain his composure, Jaxon helped him to his feet.

Fortunately, there were still no teachers on their way to send Andy and Jaxon to elementary school prison camp. It appeared the teachers hadn't seen the crazy stunt, and if Andy could walk and talk without appearing too damaged, they may get out of this mess without losing playground rights for the rest of their lives. Jaxon, being the most popular kid in class, put his entire reputation on the line by sticking around with this new kid, whom everyone was now treating like a diseased rodent. He also put his reputation with the teachers as a well-behaved kid on the line by being seen with the one who had fallen from the top of the jungle gym.

Andy became instantly and forever loyal to Jaxon and would never forget how he had treated him that day on the playground. They became inseparable best friends and would grow up always watching out for one another.

Recess was over that day, and the kids were all heading back to the building. Even though he had lost the race, Jaxon had once again found his flashy smile, which all the teachers noticed. The teachers all loved Jaxon. With Tim and Amanda being so involved in the church and community, everyone knew them and their son as well. Jaxon's teacher leaned over and said, "Almost got him today, Jax. You were so close. You ran like a Bulldog."

Jaxon looked up and asked, "Like a Bulldog? I'm an Angel." he exclaimed. Jaxon was a giant fan of the East Mississippi Angels, because that was the team his dad had rooted for his whole life. While Tim was still uncertain about his future, he had made up his mind that if he was going to play college ball, he would have gone to East Mississippi University. Even with the self-announcement of being "an Angel," the nickname "Bulldog" stuck with him for the next few years.

Jaxon was just like his dad in being able to make others laugh. The teacher kept picking at him about being a Bulldog as they approached the school building. Jaxon said, "Even if I was a dog, I wouldn't be an ugly Bulldog. Man, those rascals are ugly!"

The teacher began laughing, and he made a few more comments to keep the joke going. Jaxon, being a chip off the ol' block, loved to make people laugh. He was smiling from ear to ear as he approached the front door of the school building because of the laughter coming from his teacher.

There was another student holding the door for everyone, and Jaxon decided to introduce his new friend to another classmate. Andy was trying to make a good impression with the other students so they would like him, but nobody had even noticed him until he was with Jaxon. As they approached the young door holder, Jaxon said, "Let me introduce you to my new friend, Andy! Andy … uhhh … Hey Andy, what's your last name?"

Andy was really nervous about meeting someone new as he cautiously said, "Andrew Fish …"

Before he could finish getting his name out, Jaxon exclaimed, "This is Andy Fish!" He then surprisingly turned his head towards Andy and said, "Fish? Dude, I'm a Bull! I reckon we are both critters!"

Andy continued with a nervous, shaky voice. "Fisher … Andrew Fisher, is my name."

Jaxon started laughing and said, "Well, little Fish, you're all right by me. My name is Jaxon Bull, and Mrs. Johnson just called me a Bulldog.'"

Andy was obviously not the confident, athletic, energetic kid Jaxon was, but he had more in him than he had ever known he had before. Spending time with Jaxon, he became accepted. He never reached the popularity of his new buddy, but he was no longer shunned and picked on as sport for the others. Jaxon instilled a confidence in Andy that had never existed before. The first week he was in his new school, Jaxon took him under his care. They played well together, and Jaxon seemed to treat him like a little brother. He looked after him and introduced him to their classmates. He walked Andy through the classroom and announced, "This is Fish! He's new here. He talks too much, but he's very nice, I reckon."

Andy didn't know what to say or do. He just allowed Jaxon to do all the talking. He was willing to walk from student to student with Jaxon, as if he were part of show-and-tell, but Andy still didn't have the nerve to speak. Just walking around in class was far more than he had ever allowed himself to do before. He always wanted to stay away from any attention, because the only attention he had ever received in class before was being ridiculed and the butt of all the jokes.

Andy never was a big talker. In fact, he barely said two words during those first couple of months in his new town. That didn't seem to matter to Jaxon. Jaxon could talk enough for both of them. Jaxon was always confident and charismatic.

Jaxon took it upon himself, even at an early age, to ask people about their relationship with Jesus. He obtained his ability to interact with others from his dad. Tim was such a charismatic gentleman that people absolutely adored him. Tim loved people.

Amanda was a wonderful young woman who always cared about people's salvation. Tim lured them in with his charm, and Amanda captured their hearts with her love for Jesus and her desire to introduce others to Him. Jaxon naturally picked up on this quality through his youth. Because he liked to play and get rowdy, he was constantly disrupting Sunday school classes with students his own age.

His parents normally had to take Jaxon with them into the Sunday school classes they taught. This practice really helped Jaxon's self-assurance grow. With Tim working with the junior high kids regularly and coteaching them in Sunday school class with Amanda, Jaxon was constantly around the older kids. At his young age, he picked up tendencies that were typically only shown in kids much older than he. He was mature beyond his years in some aspects of his life, and teaching others about Jesus was no different. His avenue of acceptance was typically through sports. He was much younger, a third-grader hanging out with junior high kids, but he was always allowed to play in the gym with them, because he could athletically hang with them quite well.

Andy had been living in Mississippi for quite a few months when Jaxon finally told him, "You have to go to church with me this Sunday." Andy had always turned him down in the past, but this time Jaxon told him he had to go. He didn't present it as a question this time. What was different? Jaxon knew he wanted Andy to learn more about Jesus, and it bothered his heart that his friend wouldn't attend.

Truthfully, Andy was too afraid and intimidated to go to church. He was worried there would be kids there he wouldn't know. Kids wouldn't know he was with Jaxon, and the criticism would start all over. He was worried that he wouldn't fit in. He just knew people would know he didn't know what to do or what to say, and they would make fun of him. He didn't want to have Jaxon think less of him by showing him he really didn't belong. Jaxon was a good protector of Andy, but Andy believed that if Jaxon was challenged by older, newer kids, he would turn on him.

Jaxon again said, "You have to go!" Andy never asked why or said no. He just stood there, like he normally did, and stared intently at Jaxon. Jaxon had already given up on waiting for responses from his smaller, nontalkative friend. Andy spoke from time to time, but it was always when he felt like it, not just when others wanted him to speak. Most people in their class were unsure what Andy even sounded like, because he rarely spoke at school. Jaxon knew Andy would love it at church and begin to learn more about Jesus, if he could just get Andy to go with him.

He had to be bold. He had to come up with a reason even Andy couldn't resist.

Andy didn't want to let Jaxon down in any way. Jaxon told him that some of the kids at church had challenged him to a basketball game and that he had been told he could pick any teammate he wanted. He said, "I need you to play on my team, Fish. I can't do this without you!"

Andy looked up at him with a confused expression, because Jaxon was such a popular kid and always had the best players to choose from. Why on earth would he choose him? Jaxon had never seen Andy play basketball before and really didn't even know whether he knew how to play. He had played with Andy enough to know that, though he was small, he was extremely quick. He hoped, at the very least, that it wouldn't be a total embarrassment. He felt confident that if he could just somehow get him there, he could get him involved with church.

Jaxon had enough of a realistic view of the competition to know that the only way they were going to win was if his dad was on their team. After all, it was third-graders against junior-high kids. Even with his impressive athletic abilities, victory wasn't in their future. His goal wasn't to win the basketball game. His goal was to win Fish to Christ. That challenge was much longer and more difficult than third-graders against junior-high kids in basketball.

# 6
# A Mother's Wisdom

Fish is the first student trainer on the scene. Despite the emotional connection he has with the player, he is extremely professional and allows the full-time trainers to do their jobs while he continues to hold Jaxon's head in place. As he looks into his friend's eyes and tries to instill a sense of security for Jaxon, he worries he will begin to cry if Jaxon doesn't show progress soon.

Jaxon is still lying flat on his back and has yet to move a muscle. His friend is down, but Andy has seen this violent scene once before. He knows this could be serious, but he also knows his friend is "The Bull" and is stronger than anyone he knows or has ever heard of before.

Now Jaxon more clearly hears the voice of his friend. He is already calm, but his buddy's voice provides an extra level of peace. He hears Fish ask, "Can you hear me?" It sounds like Fish is a million miles away, but he can, in fact, hear him. He can barely make out what he is saying, and he just looks at Fish with a slight smile. He is trying, but it isn't quite like that first smile he'd flashed to Fish on that day in the third grade, when little Andy wouldn't respond to him.

*Why does he keep hollering and not listening to me?* Not aware that he is not speaking, Jaxon wonders why his friend, who for so much of their young lives barely spoke, won't shut up for one second to let him talk. He is frustrated that Fish does not seem to be listening to him, so he momentarily shifts his eyes away from his friend.

Because Jaxon is lying on his back, unable to move his head, he is very limited in what he can see. One of Jaxon's teammates is standing in a perfect spot, holding his helmet where Jaxon can see the reflection of another teammate's shoes out of the corner of his eye. His thinks back to his childhood, when he had begged his mom for a new pair of shoes, which were popular and ridiculously expensive.

"Please! I really need these shoes," Jaxon pleaded as he held up the newest version of the basketball shoes the other kids were wearing on his church league basketball team.

"Tell me, Son, why do you need those?" Amanda asked her seven-year-old son as they stood in the middle of the shoe store.

"I'll play better if I have these. I really need 'em!"

Amanda looked down at her son. "Why do you think that? You are already taller than everyone on your team *and* the leading scorer. I don't think it would be fair if those shoes made you better. Besides, these are a lot less expensive." She held up another pair of basketball shoes.

Jaxon continued to plead his case. "Mom, nobody wears those! Everyone is wearing these! These are the ones I *need*. If I can't have these, everyone will laugh at me."

"Son, we can't afford those shoes. We don't have the kind of money your friends' parents have. You can't have everything they have. We are able to get you some new basketball shoes, but they can't be that expensive. You need to pick some other ones."

"Why are my friends' parents better than us?"

Amanda took this time to sit down on the shoe store bench, where she could be closer to her son. She smiled at him, took a deep breath, and calmly asked him to stand closer to her. He slowly walked over toward his mother and gently placed the costly shoe on the ground at her feet. Jaxon carefully stepped between his mother's legs and put his hands on each of her knees, as if to brace for the bad news. He had his head down and knew he had said something wrong.

"Son, one person isn't better than another. God loves all of us the same. You know this. We have talked about this many times. Right?"

Jaxon slowly raised his head and looked at his mother. "Yes, ma'am."

"The type of shoes a person wears isn't what makes a person good or bad. Most of your friends have parents who are older than your dad and me, and they got married later in life. They are a little farther along than we are, but that doesn't make them better than us. Yes, some of them have better jobs. Some of them have more money or bigger houses. Jax, you need to always remember that where someone's mailbox is sitting doesn't determine the type of person they are. A zip code is only a number that goes on mail, not a character builder or definer. It's what's on the inside of each of us and the choices we make that determine what kind of person we are. Do you understand?"

"Yes, ma'am."

"All right then. Tell me what I mean."

Jaxon had never enjoyed having to back up his answer and always hoped to just nod and be done with it. He wasn't off the hook just yet. Both Amanda and Tim always took every opportunity to instill life lessons into Jaxon, especially when he presented such golden opportunities as this. Jaxon looked at his mother and thought for a moment about his response.

He bent over to grab the shoe, raised it where she could clearly see it again, and said, with a disappointed expression, "I ain't gettin' these shoes!"

Amanda laughed. "That's right. But you know that's not what I meant. Tell me what else you understand about what we just discussed."

Jaxon dropped the shoe by his side. "You and Daddy are just as good as everyone else."

Amanda smiled. "Who else is just as good as everyone else?"

Jaxon raised his eyebrows and asked with a little doubt in his voice, "Me?"

"That's right. You are just as good as everyone else, even if you don't have the same shoes as everyone else. Now, let's keep huntin until we find some shoes we can both agree on. Deal?"

Jaxon smiled and nodded as he and his mother continued walking around the store. "I love you, Mom," Jaxon said as he playfully leaned into her, and she wrapped her arm around him. "When we get some more money, then can I have those shoes?"

"I love you too, Son," Amanda replied. "And no, we are not getting those shoes, so you need to just let it go."

Jaxon seemed disappointed. "Why don't we have any money?"

"We *do* have money. We just aren't going to spend it on shoes that are too expensive. Just because you *can* buy something doesn't mean you *should* buy it. Just because you have enough money to buy something doesn't mean you can afford to buy something."

Jaxon looked very confused as he raised his head where he could see his mother. "I don't understand."

"Jaxon, we don't have a lot of money, but we do have money. I am trying to instill financial responsibility into you now before you have money of your own. We sometimes have to work extra hard to get special things, but we always have *enough* money. That's how we buy food, clothing, gas. It's how we pay the bills, pay our tithe, and live in our house. We don't have a lot of *extra* money, so we must choose where we spend our money and how much we spend on certain things. If I can buy the same item for one dollar as I can for two dollars, which one do you think I should buy?"

Jaxon thought for a minute, as if he were getting asked a trick question. "I think you should by the one for two dollars if you got enough money."

"Why do you think that?"

"Because the one for two dollars is better."

"Why do you think that?"

"If one of them is one dollar and the other is two dollars, the two-dollar one is better because it costs more. Right?"

Amanda stopped, turned toward Jaxon, and said, "You missed an important part of what I said, Jax. I said, they are the same. They have different prices, but they are the same."

Amanda put her hands on Jaxon's shoulders and leaned in to emphasize her words. "I want you to understand this now. You will discover in life that there are a lot of things that may appear at first glance to be better or worse because of what someone else says or the value someone else has placed on it. Living a good life requires you to exert a little effort to discover what is good, what is bad, what is overrated, what is undervalued, or whatever. You can't always trust that because someone labels something or someone for you that his or her label is accurate or that you should believe what others say you should believe. It's a really good habit to dig deeper and discover things for yourself.

"Not only with things but especially with people. You will have people in your life try to tell you that someone is good or no good. You need to always invest in people. Invest your own time in people to discover who they are and what you can offer them."

"You mean what they can offer me?"

"No," Amanda continued, "I mean, what you can offer others. I love you, and I will always love you. I want you to live your life in a way that will make me and your dad proud of you. Don't be selfish, Son. Don't just try to see what others can do for you but learn what you can do for others. If you live your life serving others, you will have a great life. You may not be rich or famous, but you will be loved.

"If you think someone already has everything and you believe you can offer them nothing, you need to keep diggin. If someone appears to have everything and they don't know Jesus, they don't have anything that will really last. If they do know Jesus, you can at least offer them your kindness. You need to always treat everyone with kindness and respect. No matter what other people may say about someone, you should take the time to discover their hearts and who they really are. People will surprise you, Jax. Some will surprise you in a negative way, but the great thing about people is, if you put in the effort, most everyone can show you something good about themselves.

"Your dad and I believe in you, Son. We believe you are a good and loving person. We have seen you display love so many times, and we are so proud of you for how you treat others. We believe you will be a good man when you grow up. You can change the world! Do you know that?"

Never taking his eyes off his mother, Jaxon said, "I don't know."

"You can!" Amanda exclaimed. "You can do anything you want to do. If you work hard and do things the right way, you can do anything you want to do in this life. Just make sure what you want is good, honest, and lines up with God's word, and God will reward your hard work and faithfulness. Things may not always work out the way you planned, but you will realize that if you let God lead, He will always show you that His plan is far better than ours could ever be. If we trust Him with our plans, He will not let us down."

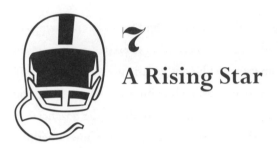

# 7

# A Rising Star

Jaxon, still believing he is responding back to Fish, is in shock. His body is not responding in any way he believes it is. He isn't fully aware of what was going on yet. He just knows Fish is in his face, shouting like he had lost his mind. Fish was always quick, so he easily outran all the other trainers and the coaches to where Jaxon was helplessly lying on the freshly manicured turf.

BJ's focus is solely on his fallen friend. BJ is a strong, physical, and godly presence on the sidelines, and he is working as an intern with the Fellowship of Christian Athletes (FCA). His assignment is with the student athletes of the EMU Angels. He is a regular figure around all the male and female, EMU athletes, because of his role with the Fellowship of Christian Athletes. But it wasn't that long ago when BJ wouldn't have had anything to do with what revolved around Christians.

Jaxon was a freshman in high school and really developing into a mature athlete. It was the third game of the season but only their first home game. Only three games into the season, Jaxon had already made a name for himself on the varsity football team. Because of his size, strength, and speed, he had earned the starting position as the team's kick returner.

It was the opening kickoff of the game, and Jaxon was receiving the ball deep in his own end zone. He was always so excited to be involved in the action that he sometimes let his enthusiasm get the better of him. Even against the coaches' demands, he brought the ball out of the end zone every time he received the kick. The problem the coaches had in telling him to not do that was that Jaxon usually made something amazing happen when he had the ball in his hands.

Jaxon had already become recognized as a talented kick returner. In this particular instance, he caught the ball deep in the end zone and sprinted down the field with the ball in his hand when another player blindsided him. The opposing player, sprinting full speed down the field, leaped into the air and smashed the crown of his helmet into the side of Jaxon's helmet. Jaxon was brutally knocked to the ground.

Everyone in the stands thought for certain he had been knocked out of the game. His teammates, ready to recover the fumble, all scrambled toward him. The players and the fans were amazed that Jaxon, lying lifelessly on the ground, was still holding onto the ball.

Because Jaxon was so close to the sidelines, Fish, a student manager on the high school team during his freshman year, was the first person to reach him. He looked down at his friend and wondered whether he was alive. Fish dropped to his knees, smacked his friend on the helmet a few times, and shouted, "Are you okay?" Needless to say, the team's athletic trainer wasn't happy at the sight of Fish's actions to the motionless player.

Jaxon opened his eyes, smiled, and raised the ball in the air. The whole crowd erupted with cheers. Jaxon had to remain sidelined the rest of the game, but his legend grew even stronger. That was also the very first moment BJ started to feel any kind of respect for Jaxon.

For every sport, all the coaches in town wanted Jaxon on their team. Tim was an enormously proud father. His son was the only ninth-grader guaranteed to start on the varsity team. Everyone wanted to stop and talk to him about his son and football. They said things like "a chip off the ol' block" and "just like his daddy." Tim swelled with pride each time. He never talked about his past sporting experiences but always wanted to make it about his son. Amanda typically chimed in with things like, "Don't give him the big head."

Amanda wasn't very interested in talking about her son playing football though. She was terrified about him playing the violent sport as a high schooler. He was only in the ninth grade and would be playing against seniors. In her mind, this situation had disaster written all over it. She didn't see him as a six-foot, 190-pound future stud athlete. She only saw her "baby" among a bunch of people who wanted to hurt him.

In reality, as a freshman, Jaxon was already bigger than most of the players on the team. She had no desire to watch him play. She couldn't watch. She couldn't even force herself to catch glimpses of his greatness. She went to all his games with Tim, but just like at the hospital when he was bleeding at three years old, she couldn't watch. When Jaxon was on the field, she only listened while praying with her head down as she sat on the bleachers next to Tim. If the pressure became too much, she listened from the parking lot on the radio of their old car. Even in his junior-high playing days, both parents were always there and supportive, but only one of them could actually see the amazing athleticism being displayed by such a young and rare talent.

Jaxon wouldn't have the opportunity to go to high school in the town of Tishomingo, where he had grown up. Years ago, the original high schools of Tishomingo High, Iuka High, Burnsville High, and Belmont High had been consolidated into just two schools. Now there is only Tishomingo County High School (TCHS), located about ten miles up the road in Iuka, and Belmont High School, just a few miles south of Tishomingo, in the town of Belmont. Tim had gone to TCHS, where he earned the nickname "Bulldozer" as a standout star in baseball, basketball, and football. When the time was right, Jaxon had to make his choice of which school to attend.

He could go to Belmont, who had been the more dominant team as of late or go to his parents' old school and follow in his dad's footsteps. Both were good schools that could provide a solid education. He had coaches, classmates, teammates, community members, and others all trying to convince him to go to one school or the other. The entire town of Tishomingo knew what he could do for or, worse, against their favorite team. All the kids he had grown up playing with and against also knew. They unquestionably didn't want to play against him.

Jaxon wanted to win, but he also wanted to compete against the best. Just like on the playground, he always looked for the biggest challenge and toughest competition. TCHS hadn't been that good the few years before, but they definitely played against more difficult competition and bigger schools than the smaller Belmont. He knew there was a possibility he could start right away for either team. Belmont was small, so they needed the numbers. TCHS was bigger but needed his skills. He wasn't sure what position he would play but believed he would play somewhere right away.

The coaches at Belmont frequently spoke to Jaxon and/or his parents every chance they could get. After church one day, the head coach at Belmont stopped and spoke to Jaxon. He gave a similar salespitch that other coaches at Belmont had given Jaxon before. Because it was a small town, everyone knew everyone already so there was rarely introductions or formality.

"Hey, Jaxon. How ya doin', bud?"

"Great, Coach. How are you?"

"Fine. Fine. I was curious if you knew where you're going yet? Your freshman year is getting close."

"No, sir. Not yet.

"Let me tell you this, Jaxon. With your size, we could really use you on the offensive *and* defensive line as you develop. We would want to bulk you up so you could clear some serious lanes for our power-running game. At your size and age, we can foresee you being a dominant force on the offensive line and a wrecking ball at defensive end by the eleventh grade. We figure that with your speed, we could use you right away as a kick *and* punt returner to protect our running back from all the extra hits. I know Tish County has talked to you too, but that's a mighty fine offer for your first year of high school ball."

This time was no different, he responded politely and with no hint of commitment. "Thanks, Coach. That is a great offer and gives me a lot to think and pray about."

Because he was a young man of faith, he prayed all summer about his decision. He prayed about it a lot. By this age, he was very solid in his faith and disciplined in his prayer life. Following his parents' footsteps and good example, Jaxon had become very active in the church and the community. He served in the community wherever he found people needing the help of a strong young man. He went on mission trips and embraced his role as a leader among his peers. He never did any of this to seem cool, to gain favor with others, to convince his elders he was more mature than his friends, or to do anything other than with pure, selfless motives. In fact, most of the time Jaxon didn't want any of his friends to know what he was doing during his spare time. He had already been accused by older kids in the past that he was only pretending or kissing up.

His examples were Jesus and his parents. It was his parents who had instilled in him the love for Jesus and others. Jaxon never really went through a rebellious stage in life. He was always a good kid, a good student, and a very hard worker. He saw and lived the example his parents modeled, and he wanted nothing more than to please them. His parents had always worked so hard to serve others, and they never did a selfish thing for themselves during their entire lives. Jaxon noticed and appreciated this fact, even from a young age.

Regardless of Tim and Amanda having Jaxon at such a young age, the townspeople of Tishomingo never treated them like kids raising a kid. They were two of the hardest-working and pleasant people anyone had ever met. Tim always played with all the kids, had fun with all the kids, and got in trouble with all the kids. He had done this regularly when Jaxon was young, but nearly everyone considered him to be the best dad and husband in town.

It seemed as if the whole town felt the Bulls were part of their family and loved all three of them as if they were their own kids and grandkid. Deep down everyone knew that regardless of where Jaxon chose to go to high school, the town would stay supportive of the Bulls. There were constant jokes about how they were willing to kick their support into high gear for Jaxon if he went to the school of their preference.

# 8

# A Gentle Nudge of Encouragement

BJ, while representing the Fellowship of Christian Athletes on the sidelines, drops to one knee, bows his head, and begins to pray for Jaxon. At this point, BJ is the only person praying. From where he was standing, he can tell the injury is bad, and he can see exactly who is lying on the ground. He knows the best way he can help his friend is to ask God to get involved.

BJ and Jaxon didn't always have such a great relationship. Their now, rock-solid friendship, had a rocky start. Before Jaxon chose what high school he would attend, the coaches at Tishomingo County High School told him he could play anywhere he wanted, but there would be some serious competition for the positions he wanted to play. TCHS had a lot of players to choose from, but none were stars at their positions. There wasn't significant competition at any position except one on offense and one on defense. The same player held both. Their best player the year before was their quarterback and strong safety.

Brandon "BJ" James was by far TCHS's best and most promising athlete in years. He was the best athlete the north end of the county had seen since the legendary "Bulldozer." Jaxon's dad had been the last great prospect from Tishomingo County. The good ones in that area were from Belmont. BJ was a very strong and successful athlete, and he was considered by far the best college prospect in the area. BJ was fast, strong, smart, and popular. In a lot of ways, he was an older version of Jaxon. Shortly after BJ moved to Tishomingo, after only a few pickup basketball games in the city park of Iuka, he became the most popular kid in town.

With his six-foot, four-inch, 210-pound frame, he stood out in school and in sports. BJ was new to the school system, but when the coaches at TCHS saw his size and athletic ability, there was no question he could be the team leader and the one who could improve their record. He did just that. He led TCHS to six wins that season as the quarterback. At first glance, the record may not have seemed that impressive to most people, but they had won only four games during the previous two seasons combined.

BJ and his family moved to Tishomingo the summer before his junior year. Jaxon, only an eighth- grader at the time, had already caught the attention of BJ. The folks in town told BJ he needed to get to know Jaxon and help him grow as an athlete, because he was "going to be the next big star 'round here." BJ was a cocky and ambitious guy who didn't care at all about helping an eighth-grader in any way possible.

As self-assured as he was, Jaxon never seemed to notice that BJ wanted nothing to do with him. He saw him from time to time around town and a lot out at the state park, when he went to work with Tim.

BJ hadn't yet even met Jaxon, but he knew he didn't like him. In BJ's mind, Jaxon was just a kid, and he was a star in high school. He continued to hear about Jaxon during his entire junior year, because they both lived in the town of Tishomingo. He spent a lot of his free time in the town of Iuka, where the high school was located. He considered Iuka "his town" and didn't really care for the smaller, simpler Tishomingo.

As TCHS's quarterback, BJ had what everyone considered to be a very successful junior year. With the six wins and his impressive abilities, he also brought a lot of attention to the team and even more to himself. He was gaining a reputation as a guy who could get any girl he wanted. The problem was, he wanted them all. BJ didn't have the moral and spiritual background or work ethic Jaxon had and was interested only in having fun.

Jaxon made up his mind about what school he was going to attend and why. He had spent the entire summer working out as hard as he could because his goal was not to just get some playing time or even start but seriously contribute to the school he chose to attend. His workouts and relentless work ethic eventually became legendary and followed him everywhere he went. He had a fierce competitive nature.

He spent a lot of time at the park that summer. His dad, the head maintenance man at this point, had a lot of options at his disposal, which could provide his son with great and creative possibilities for working out. There were miles of trails where Jaxon spent his time running sprints and doing agility work and body weight workouts. His dad, called "Coach" by his son as well, didn't want Jaxon using free weights yet, so he rarely ever did anything other than body weight. Tim also told him that swimming would put him in the best possible shape. When he finished his workouts on the trails, he took a lunch break with his dad and then visited the elderly groups that got together every day at the old park pavilion.

Jaxon learned a lot about people. He learned a great deal about how to listen by visiting those "old farts," as he affectionately called them. He loved visiting them, and they loved having him around. He was just a kid, but they treated him like he was an adult most of the time.

He was always willing to help them with whatever they needed. He sat and listened to stories from long ago by the older, wiser community members. He loved hearing stories about his dad playing sports. He loved hearing stories about his mother being the "most wonderful girl who ever lived." It always made him laugh when the old folks made fun of each other. He loved above all else to hear stories about how and when each of these delightful people came to know Jesus and that someone cared enough about them to lead them to a life of salvation with the Lord. That was great motivation for him to strive to always be a positive witness for others.

BJ knew that during the summer everyone would be scattered around and that if he didn't improvise, it would be very difficult to have as much fun as he had during the school year. So, being the ladies' man, he was, he planned ahead and believed the best way to find the women was to have the women come to him. He knew there was one place where he could always keep his eyes on the best possible options. He became a lifeguard at Tishomingo State Park. It was at that park where BJ really began to dislike Jaxon.

It was usually just before two p.m. every day when Jaxon showed up to the pool, always shortly followed by Fish. Jaxon did his morning workouts by himself, and then Andy met him for his afternoon workouts at the pool. Jaxon convinced Andy that he needed to train during the summer to be able to get in good enough shape for the football tryouts that year. Jaxon knew Andy wasn't big enough to be too much of a standout at practices, but Andy loved playing sports, competing, and working hard with Jaxon.

Jaxon knew that for Andy to really make an impact, it would have to be because of his conditioning. He repeatedly said, "We can't get tired. We can't let 'em see us suckin wind like the rest of the freshmen are gonna be. Coach D says, 'Every year, these knuckleheads look so wore out that you'd think these kids had one of their lungs stolen in the middle of the night just before the first practice.' We can't let that be us, dude. We gotta be in better shape than anyone else. You gotta swim this summer like a fish. We gotta swim all summer and be in better shape than anyone else."

Andy didn't have anyone in the neighborhood talking about him playing football in high school. He was going to have to earn his way, and it was going to be harder for him than for anyone else. Really, everyone just knew Fish as "Jaxon's buddy, Fish." He didn't have much of an identity of his own. He always followed Jaxon around, and Jaxon always looked after him. Everyone liked him, but nobody really expected much out of the undersized, soft-spoken "shadow of the Bull." He had a lot of toughness about him but was always naturally weaker than most of the others. What he did have, though, was the will to work and succeed. They showed up every day at the pool, ready to swim.

BJ had to watch these goofy kids all summer long get out there and "waste their time swimming" at the pool when he knew "real football" took place on a field. BJ wasn't interested in training hard during the summer, because even after getting a suntan and drinking beer all summer, he was still going to be the best player on the team next season. BJ would be going into his senior year, and he already had college recruiters pursuing him to play quarterback for their teams. He had several head coaches make personal visits, trying to get a head start on the competition before his senior year.

Playing college football, for BJ, was definitely going to happen. BJ was naturally gifted with great passing accuracy and a rocket arm. The biggest problem he'd had last year was that the offensive line wasn't very decent. Most of the big, strong kids in school, who could easily defend the line, were more interested in deer hunting during football season than in playing football. Football just wasn't a big interest for too many of the young'uns in that area. More kids played baseball, because it didn't disrupt deer hunting season.

With his mirrored sunglasses and a dark suntan, BJ was sitting shirtless in the lifeguard stand with one leg over the handrail, watching Jaxon and Andy swim laps. He became bored watching them swim, so when they took their first rest, BJ decided to engage in a little sport with Jaxon.

"Bulldog?" BJ said, referring to one of Jaxon's many nicknames. "You don't strike me as a Bulldog. With your pathetic attempts at swimming laps, you strike me as more of a Bullfrog." Jaxon finally had BJ acknowledge him face-to-face, but it wasn't to say he wanted to play ball with him next season.

After that moment, he picked on Jaxon and Andy most of the summer. Jaxon didn't seem to mind as long as BJ didn't bother Andy too much. He usually had a snappy comeback, accompanied with a smile.

"Bullfrog? I like that!" Jaxon said. "I'm a Bullfrog, and this is my buddy, Fish." He pointed toward Andy, who was actually a surprisingly good swimmer. "My dad and I watched you play a lot last year, and you sure can sling that pigskin. My dad thinks if you had a little more time in the backfield, you'd be All State. If I go to Tish County, I'd sure love to catch a touchdown from you."

BJ wasn't too impressed with the compliment. He had thought for sure the Bullfrog name would aggravate Jaxon, but little did he know Jaxon had heard that one before. He had heard them all.

"Catch a touchdown from me? Not gonna happen, kid. You'll just be a freshman, and I'm a senior. I'll be throwin' bombs in college before you ever even get on the field. Maybe you can bring me some water this season after I throw some TDs to our actual starters. I plan on throwing a lot of 'em, and I heard you're kinda fast for a wimp, so you can rush that water right out to me."

Jaxon said, "Man, I'll do whatever the coach wants me to do. If he asks me to be a water boy, you go ahead and bet. I'll work to be the best water boy you ever saw."

Growing up around all the older kids, he had always been the butt of jokes and sarcasm. He knew how to handle bullies and deflect jokes with the best of them. His parents had always taught him not to let stuff bother him, and the best revenge would be not to let anyone ever see him or her get under his skin. He'd had plenty of opportunities to learn how to handle negative comments over the years. There was no way someone could rattle him if all the comments were directed solely at him. It really took bothering someone he loved for Jaxon to get fired up. BJ just wasn't quite aware of that yet.

Jaxon knew that even if BJ was continuously mean to him and Fish, BJ had a lot of potential. He could tell people really liked BJ and that he was extremely talented. He seemed to be a natural leader and could get anyone to listen to him. That was another reason he was such a good quarterback. He commanded the attention of other players very well in the huddle. Jaxon tried a lot that summer to become friends with BJ, but the star quarterback wanted nothing to do with him or Fish.

Every day when Jaxon arrived at the pool, he approached BJ and said things like, "Wanna throw this afternoon when you get off work? I'll be glad to catch for ya."

He even tried to invite BJ to church. "We are havin' a cool service this weekend at church. You should come. We can play basketball in the church gym afterward."

BJ never agreed to any of it. He always said something like, "I'll be gettin' some attention from the ladies," or "I'm gonna get drunk and actually have a good time." There was never a simple "No thanks, I've got plans" response from BJ. He always tried to be a nuisance to Jaxon and Andy.

Things really got ugly one day that summer when everyone was showing off at the pool, going off the diving board. BJ was the head lifeguard and was considered the best diver there. Jaxon learned a lot by watching the older kids go off the board over the years and was a pretty talented diver, too.

BJ had never seen Jaxon dive before; he had seen him only swim laps. BJ regularly went off the board, and people cheered and clapped for him. BJ was a very talented athlete, and he put his athleticism on full display when he was on the board. Not only was he good at football and diving; he was good at showing off.

One sunny afternoon Jaxon was relaxing and joking with Fish in the corner of the pool when someone yelled across the pool to BJ. "I bet Bullfrog can do more tricks off the board than you." All the local kids knew what Jaxon could do as a diver. They had all grown up with him and knew he could do anything athletically. He was becoming known as the "young Jim Thorpe" of Tishomingo County.

BJ just started laughing and said, "Baby Bull and his little Fish? They are guppies, not sharks. They better just keep doggie paddling over in the corner."

Everyone started laughing, and so did Jaxon. He didn't care one bit about what BJ had to say. He was there to get in better shape, not to dive. Diving was just for fun. He was there to improve.

The same kid who had requested a diving competition to occur between the two star athletes wouldn't give up so easily. He hollered again, "I bet we can bounce Fish a mile high off the board."

One of the tricks everyone loved to do was "bounce" each other off the board. This was done by a heavier person getting behind a lighter person on the board to help spring him or her into the air. The first diver on the board would jump in the air, and just before landing on the board, the second diver, typically a heavier person, would hold onto the rails and bounce as hard as he or she could to spring the first diver even farther into the air. This trick was typically not allowed off the board, because it resulted in someone getting hurt half the time. Of course, there were lots of things consistently happening at that pool when the park manager wasn't around that weren't allowed.

BJ had a bad habit of showing up to work hungover from the night before, and sometimes he was still slightly drunk. Every now and then, he went out to the parking lot on slow days and took a few hits off a joint with some of the older local guys, who had dropped out of high school and never gone to college. These were the types of guys who didn't care about their futures and were constantly in trouble with the law. He considered these guys very fun, and they always could get beer for him and his buddies. Today was one of the days when he would slip out and drink with his buddies when he was supposed to be watching the pool. A lot of the guys had the tendency of sneaking into the park to drink beer and play in the creek, but today they decided to hang out at the pool. BJ had allowed them in the pool area without paying, or they would have just gone to the creek instead.

"What about it, little Fish stick?" BJ said to Fish. "Let us shoot you across the pool." All BJ's buddies began to laugh and try to get Andy to join in the fun.

"Come on, runt, it will be awesome. I bet we can launch you across the whole pool," shouted one of the older, slightly intoxicated kids.

Everyone took turns shouting for Fish, but he didn't want to do it and was becoming anxious from all the unwanted attention. Andy didn't like what was happening at this moment. He was ready to leave, and Jaxon could tell the teasing was really rattling him.

Jaxon finally said, "How about I give it a try?" as he climbed out of the pool.

Jaxon was much bigger than Fish but still smaller than BJ at this point, so it made sense he would be the one to get bounced.

BJ condescendingly said, "That's the spirit, little fella."

Even as a soon-to-be ninth-grader, with his tanned and muscular physique, Jaxon was already beginning to look like a grown man. He was more imposing than all the other boys, with the exception of BJ. BJ was a man among boys himself. They were both very impressive looking young men. Many of the teenaged girls who went to the pool habitually stared at Jaxon and BJ, while they gossiped and worked on a tan for themselves. As they both walked toward the diving board, the two alpha males looked like prize fighters getting ready to square off before a heavily anticipated bout.

Jaxon walked confidently over to all the guys and started saying hello to everyone. As they began greeting one another, BJ had to briefly walk over to talk to one of the other lifeguards. They all knew who Jaxon was, and he had known most of them from his younger days when his dad was their coach. With him still being in school at the middle school in Tishomingo and most of these kids hanging out in Iuka or Belmont, he rarely got to see any of them.

"Man, Bull! You've gotten big," said one of the guys.

"What have you been eatin? You look like a roided-out bodybuilder!" another guy said, "I ain't seen you since Coach D was my coach."

Several of the guys acted happy to see him, because they had always liked him as a kid. With his parents' involvement with everything in town, he was practically the unofficial little brother of nearly every older kid in Tishomingo. Because these guys were all in high school or older, they really hadn't seen him much over the years, and he had grown quite a bit. When they went out to the park, most of these guys normally went to the creek, not to the pool, where Jaxon worked out. It was a lot easier to get caught drinking at the pool than on the creek bank. Out there they could do whatever they wanted with little fear of getting caught.

"Who's gonna bounce me?" Jaxon asked.

One guy was already standing on the board and said, "Come on up, bruh. I'll do it."

Jaxon was a little heavier than the guy who planned on bouncing him, but he still was able to get pretty high in the air and did a simple dive into the water. A few others took turns going off the board, and Jaxon bounced a few guys too. He was really good at it, because he had good timing and was heavy enough. They were all having a harmlessly good time until BJ decided he wanted to bounce Jaxon.

"Stealing a bounce" was what they did to make someone fall into the water without being able to do the intended dive. The lead diver expected the guy behind him to help him bounce, but rather than bouncing, he instead held down the board at the right time to prevent there being much spring in the board. This always led to a laugh from everyone except the person diving. It was also a good way to get someone hurt. There had been a few knee injuries over the years with that stunt, and people typically did that to others only to annoy them.

Jaxon took his position on the board, and BJ got directly behind him. This was really the first moment they had joined together, doing anything as a "team." Jaxon drew a deep breath and gracefully started toward the end of the board. BJ allowed him to get a few steps ahead and began moving like a skilled hunter, stalking his prey. As Jaxon approached the end of the board, he drew his left knee up to his chest as he sprang into the air. On his way down, he expected the board to be ready for his massive jump, but the board was low and completely still. BJ had "stolen the bounce." While Jaxon was in the air, BJ grabbed the handrails tightly and pushed the board down, stopping it completely with his feet and the weight of his body. This caused Jaxon to land awkwardly and fall into the pool.

The entire crowd of curious pool onlookers let out a collective "Ouuuuuu" as Jaxon plunged into the water. Some people said things like, "Boy, he's gonna be fightin mad" and "I bet that hurt," while others said, "I bet there's gonna be a fight when he gets out of the water."

BJ turned to all his tipsy buddies, laughing hysterically at the way he'd caused Jaxon to look so foolish. Most were laughing with BJ, while others curiously watched the deep end of the pool to see whether Jaxon was hurt.

As Jaxon reemerged from the depths, everyone started clapping, laughing, whispering, and/or checking on him. Jaxon was fine. He was always fine. Andy had a slight look of concern, but it was probably more a look of frustration about BJ's unsportsmanlike move.

Jaxon had a serious expression on his face, and nobody knew for sure what was about to happen. Was he going to try to fight the older, stronger quarterback? Was he going to be heard cursing for the first time? Was he going to just leave without incident? Andy knew his own limitations but wasn't afraid to go beyond them. He knew he was no match physically for BJ or his buddies, but win or lose, he was ready to fight if it came to that. BJ quickly climbed off the diving board and made his way around to where Jaxon would be climbing out of the pool.

As Jaxon neared the edge of the pool, he glanced up at BJ and said, "Brother, I hope you can do better than that. Not a lot on that bounce. I bet Fish could have gotten me higher than you just did."

Everyone started laughing aloud. Here was this young kid, who always had a swagger about him, embarrassed by a soon-to-be senior, but instead of trying to retaliate, he'd made a joke out of it. He was well composed.

BJ, someone who preferred being in control of a situation, didn't like the fact that Jaxon had handled it as well as he did and didn't back down. BJ just gave a little chuckle and said, "Yeah, I guess I missed that one. My bad."

With a devilish smile, BJ sarcastically said, "Come on back up. I'll get cha good on this one, I promise."

Jaxon, never backing down from a challenge and loving good competition (or in this case, dirty competition), decided to get back up there. He wasn't going to be easily defeated.

Jaxon climbed back up the small ladder and took his spot in front of BJ.

BJ calmly said, "Ready when you are."

Jaxon took one step ahead and grabbed the handrails very tightly. He was planning on getting a good jump, no matter how BJ tried to mess with the board.

Jaxon rocked his weight back and said, "Let's go!" as he lunged forward toward the end of the board. After his initial jump, he anticipated the board not being in position and was prepared to adjust. As he came back down for the main spring, he felt a violent shove in the middle of his back.

BJ didn't even bother messing with Jaxon's bounce but rather went straight to the source. Jaxon's head snapped back like a whiplash victim in a car wreck, and he fell awkwardly into the pool.

This wasn't what anyone expected. This seemed to be a tremendously painful and violent move against the eighth-grader. The only ones laughing this time were BJ and a few of his friends.

Andy wasn't amused. He started screaming at BJ and calling him a bully.

BJ jumped down and started toward him, and towering over him, he said, "You better shut up, Fishstick, or I'll give you a lesson in respecting your elders."

Andy said, "I'm not as big as you, but if I was, you'd get what's coming to you. You're nothing but a coward!"

BJ wasn't amused by Andy's brave attempt to defend Jaxon. He got even closer to Andy and was about to grab him when Jaxon sprang out of the water and jumped between them.

Jaxon, being quick witted and calm under pressure, simply said, "Fish! Dude, it's time to go. I'm wore out from our workout, and we have *got* to let BJ practice bouncing people, because he's the worst I've ever seen." Jaxon turned to BJ and continued his thought. "I'm just glad he can chunk a football better than he can bounce folks, or we won't win a single game next season."

Everyone, including BJ's friends, immediately started laughing. Jaxon had got him again. Not only did he not get into an altercation with BJ, but Jaxon made fun of him while complimenting him. This embarrassed and angered BJ, but it also confused him. BJ was really the only one who noticed that Jaxon had said "we" when referring to the football team at TCHS.

As Jaxon and Fish approached the exit gate of the pool, BJ quickly approached Jaxon and grabbed him by the arm. As he swung him around, he said, "Why did you say 'we'? There is no 'we' at my school. You belong at Belmont and nowhere near my school."

Jaxon looked into his eyes and calmly said, "After that, I don't think I could handle being on the opposite team as you. You hit me hard enough as it is. I sure don't want to give you any reason to abuse me more than you already have."

BJ quickly responded with, "You haven't seen abuse yet. You come to Tish County, and I'll see to it you get plenty of punishment from everyone on *my* team. If you don't go to Belmont, I'll make certain you develop a new understanding of pain."

# 9
## Unfortunate Opportunity

Now that he is finished praying, BJ stands to his feet and walks quickly along the sidelines. "Take a knee!" BJ tells many of the players who haven't noticed the injury to their teammate to get down on one knee. He is preparing several of the players, who normally pray together, to circle up and pray for Jaxon. As the players start dropping one by one to their knees, BJ remembers an occasion when someone had dropped to his knee to pray over him.

It was the last game of Jaxon's freshman year and the last game of BJ's high school football career. BJ was one of the hottest recruits coming out of high school in the entire country. He had shattered most of the Mississippi high school season passing records and several national records. He was being recruited by every big-time program in the country. He hadn't made his decision yet on which school he would attend, because he was enjoying the recruiting efforts way too much to give them up.

Jaxon had chosen Tishomingo County High School mostly because of that summer at the pool. He figured that because of BJ's ability to lead others, he believed BJ was truly a guy capable of leading others to Christ. But first he had to develop a relationship with Jesus himself. Even as a young boy going into the ninth grade, Jaxon had felt called to be part of BJ's story.

After Jaxon showed he held onto the ball on the opening kickoff of his first home game, BJ began to believe there was something special about this kid. BJ didn't let on to Jaxon that he believed this, but he did start paying closer attention to the freshman. He observed how Jaxon treated others and, more importantly, how he treated BJ at that point in life and how hard Jaxon worked to become the best. BJ always relied more on his natural abilities and rarely had to work to improve. He was just always better than everyone else, which made him lazy.

His laziness caught up with him during the last game of the season in the state championship game. He was dropping back for a pass when a massive defensive end crushed him from his blindside. It was a clean hit but a nasty one. BJ was instantly knocked unconscious and slammed into the ground. Because he was unable to protect himself on the way to the ground, he also fell violently onto his throwing shoulder.

The paramedics and the training staff placed him on the backboard and rushed him to the hospital for observation. After several rounds of tests to check for any brain trauma, the doctors began checking for other problems, which may have occurred from the game. They discovered he had mangled his throwing shoulder. There was major damage to the ligaments, muscles, and rotator cuff. He wasn't aware of how badly the shoulder was damaged, but he knew he was in a lot of pain. The doctors gave him some medicine, which knocked him back out and allowed him to sleep through the night.

When BJ woke up the next morning, the first thing he saw was the top of Jaxon's head. Jaxon was kneeled at BJ's bedside, holding his hand while praying for him. While Jaxon's eyes were still closed, BJ slowly and cautiously looked around the room but didn't see anyone else. He was still groggy from the medicine and very confused. He wondered why Jaxon was taking a nap while holding his hand. He wasn't aware that Jaxon was praying. It didn't occur to him Jaxon would even consider doing such a thing for him.

Over the course of the season, BJ had started becoming a little more cordial toward Jaxon but still hadn't gone out of his way to be nice to him or interact with him. He still took jabs at Jaxon every chance he got. He did his best to embarrass Jaxon in front of teammates, classmates, and especially the girls from school. Why would Jaxon pray for him when he had never treated Jaxon like a friend?

As BJ's senses became a little sharper, he finally spoke up. "Did you run everyone off so you could hold my hand?" BJ said to Jaxon as he pulled his hand away.

Jaxon looked up and flashed his smile. "I was wondering how long you were going to play possum in here. That was quite a lick you took last night. You remember any of it?"

BJ scanned the room again and still wondered why Jaxon was the only one there. There weren't any coaches, teammates, cheerleaders, fans, or anyone else. "Where is everyone?"

Jaxon stood up, backed away from the bed, and sat down in the chair near the wall. "Your mom was here all night with you. I got here this morning and told her I would keep an eye on you so she could go get some breakfast. She should be back any minute. She'll be glad to see you awake."

BJ was very popular in school, so he was stunned to see his room empty. Nobody had come to see him in the hospital except the one person he didn't want in his room. "Why are you here?"

"I'm here to see you," Jaxon said. "I heard most of the coaches will be by sometime today. They didn't come earlier because they had to stick around the fieldhouse after the game last night and see to it the rest of the guys were good."

BJ pushed it further. "Yeah, but why? Why are *you* here? I don't understand why *you* are here."

Jaxon, leaning back in his chair, crossed his arms and with a big smile said, "Because you can't go anywhere." BJ just looked at him with a confused and aggravated stare.

"Every time I have asked you to hang out with me, go to church with me, work out with me, throw the ball with me, or anything, you just blew me off. Now you can't shake me loose on this one. You can't get away. I can say or do anything I want in here, and you'll just have to deal with it."

BJ started squirming around in this hospital bed. "You just keep your distance. I don't need you trying to do anything weird to me."

Jaxon just started laughing. "I'm not going to do anything to you. Brother, I'm just here to keep you company."

Because BJ had lived such a selfish life, nobody was in any kind of hurry to get to the hospital and visit him. This was the first time he could remember when he didn't have a posse of followers ready to do whatever he asked. This was also his first time ever to go to the hospital, including as a visitor.

Jaxon was very comfortable around the hospital because he had grown up visiting his mom, and he loved praying with patients every chance he had to visit. As the star quarterback in town and with everyone wanting to be seen with him, BJ always appeared to be extremely popular. Now that the season was over and his chances of playing college ball had been destroyed last night, the spotlight was no longer pointed at him. It was becoming painfully obvious that his popularity was gained for very different reasons than Jaxon's. He was popular because of what he could do, and Jaxon was popular for how he treated others.

It was finally starting to sink in that he may be in some serious trouble. He asked Jaxon, "How bad is it?"

"Good news is, you'll be fine. You're just going to have a pretty good headache for a while. Bad news is, you still won't look as good as me."

"I don't mean my head. My arm! How bad is my arm?"

Jaxon looked at him for what seemed like ten minutes, took a deep breath, and forcefully let all his air out. "Your mom should be here any minute," Jaxon said as he tried stalling.

"Tell me!"

"Brother, it depends on what you consider bad." Jaxon paused for a moment and decided to shoot BJ straight. "The doc said you'll never be able to throw the same way again. He said he doesn't think you'll ever play ball again."

BJ was stunned. He just dropped his head and didn't say a word.

"Look, brother, I know this isn't what you want to hear right now, but my dad has taught me a lot over the years, and one thing he told me for certain is that football isn't for certain. Football is a game. Any chance we have to play the game we love we should consider an extra-special blessing from God. It will be taken away from us at some point in life, and when it does, we need to have a plan."

BJ didn't appear impressed with Jaxon's speech. He took a deep breath, his eyes began to tear up, and he stared at the ceiling. "Get out," were the only words BJ could manage for fear of crying in front of Jaxon.

Jaxon was very disappointed that he couldn't seem to get through to BJ. His entire way home, all he could think about were his failures to reach BJ. After all his efforts, it seemed BJ was never going to like him, and Jaxon wasn't used to someone disliking him so much.

"You just get in from the hospital?" Tim asked. "How's he doin'?"

"I don't know, Dad. He's in a bad place right now." Jaxon seemed exhausted in his answer. "He hates my guts, and I think I'm just making him madder than a wet hen by even being in there. I can't seem to do anything to get him to like me."

"Don't be so hard on yourself, J," Tim said as he tried to encourage his son.

"But Dad, I've tried everything. I've been nice to him! I've invited him to everything I can think of this year. I've worked my tail off at practice … every … single … day! And on top of that, I was the only person, other than his mom, who visited him in the hospital, and he still doesn't like me."

"You want some company at the party?" Tim joked.

"What party?"

"The pity party you're thowin over there. Son, is that your goal? For him to *like* you? Life isn't a popularity contest. Jesus was the greatest man who ever walked the earth, and they killed Him. He is the most talked-about person ever, and there are still people who hate Him today, and others claim He never even existed.

"If you go through this life being disappointed because not everyone likes you, you better get your Bible back open. If Jesus wasn't liked by everyone, what makes you think you will be? You need to get your priorities back on track and not be thinking about yourself. Your mother and I didn't raise you to go to hospital rooms to get people to like you. We didn't raise you to put yourself first when helping others. I don't want you to answer me. I want you to pray about my question. When you visit BJ next time, is your heart going to be where it's supposed to be?"

# 10
## Gaining Ground

By now, BJ has most of the players down on one knee. Word is spreading on the field about who exactly is lying on the ground. This is an unfamiliar sight to this squad of gridiron warriors. They are in disbelief that the Bull is down and not jumping back to his feet, ready for the next play. Some of the kneeled players are praying, and others are watching, waiting for Jaxon to be helped to his feet.

All around the field and on the field are players of different sizes, shapes, colors, and abilities. Some are breathing heavily because they are exhausted from the game. Some are seemingly holding their breath, trying to see whether Jaxon is going to be able to stand up or even move. Some players have their heads up and eyes wide open; others have their heads down with their eyes closed. Nobody is saying a word.

Jaxon's freshman season on the varsity squad was over. His team lost in the high school state championship game, their star quarterback suffered a career-ending injury, and the whole team was down in the dumps.

"Let's get to work!" Jaxon seemed eager to begin weight training the following Monday after class. The entire field house was full of players dragging around and acting like they had lost their puppies. Jaxon was already eager to start preparing for next year's repeat run at the state championship.

He worked his way up and down the locker room, slapping guys on the shoulder or back, yelling at everyone and trying to motivate all his teammates. "Let's get after it! Let's get to work! No better time to improve than right now!"

As some of his teammates started following him toward the weight room, he went from one area of the field house to the other, trying to motivate his team. Bounding through the building like an excited child, he pumped his fists in the air, flexed his muscles, and said, "Let's do this! Let's start a new win streak today!"

He was a leader, shaped and molded by his parents and the experiences they had exposed him to throughout his life. Nobody was in the mood to lift weights, but Jaxon was hungry. He was starving. He wanted to improve so badly; he couldn't wait to get stronger and better.

Nobody had ever seen anyone work out as hard as this freshman. He was the first one in the weight room and the last to leave each day. He used the sledgehammers and chains; he moved the sleds around like they were paperweights and was unbelievably strong. All the push-ups, pull-ups, sit-ups, and swimming Tim had encouraged Jaxon to do over the years were finally getting put into action in a real weight room. He was having a blast using all this "fancy equipment," which he wasn't used to using.

The coaches were amazed by this young stud. They knew from watching him during the season that his motor wouldn't just quit, but they never saw him lift weights before, because the team didn't lift during the season. They had the players long enough after school each day only for them to practice football.

Up to this point, Tim hadn't allowed Jaxon to lift weights, so this was also unfamiliar territory for him. Jaxon's "weight room" had always been his dad's workshop—chopping wood, carrying heavy items at the park, swimming, and running, jumping, and helping with manual labor jobs on mission trips and around the neighborhood. He used every opportunity to help people with yard work or chores as a workout and a chance to get better. He finally got the taste of working out in a real weight room, and he loved it. He was hooked. His fierce competitive nature made him constantly want to exceed his own personal best.

Jaxon was true to his word with BJ. He had a captive audience, so he visited BJ regularly. BJ became very depressed with his injury and the fallout that came with it. He discovered the hard way that being selfish and hateful with a lot of talent was a lot easier than being selfish and hateful with a busted throwing arm and no future in sports. He felt very alone. This was his senior year, and he was supposed to be having the time of his life, but he was miserable. He had very few visitors during his recovery. The recruiting trips stopped immediately. People weren't going out of their way to help BJ feel better, and his friends rarely interacted with him outside of being at school. Everything in his life felt empty. Everyone in his life just seemed different.

Jaxon poured his efforts into BJ. He was bound and determined to lead him to Christ before BJ graduated. At a very early age, Jaxon learned to be focused on what was ahead of him more than on what was behind him. He could see BJ's high school finish line, even if BJ had completely lost sight of where he was going. Jaxon prayed and worked extremely hard for the rest of the school year to lead BJ to Christ. Jaxon knew that once BJ was gone from Tishomingo, he may never see him again.

BJ was still a good student, even if he didn't have to work hard for his grades, so college was still in his future. He had good enough grades and test scores that he would be able to go to college if he chose that route. After his injury, he lost his desire to go to college. He didn't have a plan, and he had very little desire to think about or discuss his college prospects.

Jaxon started taking Fish along with him every chance they had to go and visit BJ. Fish was always ready to go anywhere Jaxon wanted to go and do anything he asked. Jaxon never took advantage of Fish's willingness to follow and always protected him like a little brother. At first, BJ wasn't tremendously friendly to either of the two youngsters, but after the first several visits, he started to realize they were the only visitors he was getting. After BJ was released from the hospital, Jaxon and Fish continued to show up everywhere he went. They appeared during his rehabilitation sessions with the physical therapist. They suspiciously showed up at his house and became very helpful at the exact moment BJ's mom would unload groceries or need help.

Each time Jaxon and Fish spent a little time with him, Jaxon always offered to pray for BJ before they left. Usually BJ declined the offer, but Jaxon prayed anyway. He said things like, "Well, you can just sit there. I've got some things to say to Jesus. Feel free to listen in or ignore me."

Other times he asked Fish to pray over both of them. Fish was still not much of a talker, but he had heard Jaxon and his parents pray aloud so many times; he could manage to get enough words out of his mouth to resemble a spoken prayer. He didn't act overly excited about it, but he nervously looked forward to his turn when Jaxon called on him to pray. The first several times Jaxon asked Fish to pray, it was just the two of them, with nobody else around. Jaxon knew Fish would be too nervous to pray aloud unless he gave him opportunities to comfortably practice.

Jaxon was experienced and comfortable with praying aloud for others, because he and his parents prayed together daily. They were always involved in their church, leading small groups in their home and mission trips. The Bulls were truly a family of prayer. They believed in it and lived it. From the time Jaxon could remember, his family used their knowledge, skills, and abilities to serve others. They believed their mission field was wherever they were at any given moment. They enjoyed doing foreign missions, but they couldn't afford to take several trips each year or be away from work that long. They took one foreign mission trip each year and worked hard to instill those values into Jaxon's life.

As Jaxon got older, he was allowed to start taking Fish along with him on the foreign mission field. Tim and Amanda trusted Jaxon to stay focused and not goof around with his buddy, because he had proven himself to be very serious about serving others and the Lord. He took advantage of every opportunity to help someone else and never took for granted his responsibility to represent Christ as best he could.

After constant, unannounced, and unwanted visits from Jaxon and Fish, BJ finally started revealing a softer side. It took him longer to warm up to Fish, because he rarely spoke, but he really did admire Jaxon's tenaciousness and Fish's loyalty. He never admitted it to them, but he enjoyed having the company. BJ remained crude with his interactions with the two younger boys and tried to embarrass them by talking about the older girls from school. He talked about which girl was best in bed or which ones were terrible kissers. He constantly asked them which girls they were getting physical with or who they wanted to see bare all. Each time Fish turned red and didn't say a word, and Jaxon talked his way around the subject. He never wanted to come across as judgmental, but he also didn't want to encourage BJ to continue telling them stories about his real or made-up sexual conquests.

With Jaxon's looks, having a servant's heart toward everyone he met, and being an all-star athlete and an all-around great guy, the older high school girls were all extremely aware of who he was. He experienced temptation around every corner. There were constant rumors and requests about who he was dating or should be dating, but his focus was on improvement. He wanted to improve at sports and his relationship with BJ to lead him to Christ. By the middle of his freshman year, he was already friends with everyone in school, but he had no interest in having a girlfriend.

Over the remainder of his freshman year, Jaxon repeatedly asked BJ to join him and Fish for prayer time with the Fellowship of Christian Athletes in the mornings before school started. Jaxon asked BJ every week to join him and Fish for church on Sundays or Wednesdays, but BJ always declined. BJ didn't make up excuses for why he couldn't go; he simply said, "Not interested" or "No thanks." He didn't tell Jaxon or Fish, "Maybe next time" or give any other words of encouragement to keep asking. Jaxon never relented. He continued asking as politely as he could and didn't pressure him after being rejected each time.

Jaxon just made the offer, smiled, and said, "Maybe next week!" He never gave up asking, and he never gave up on BJ.

Over the course of the spring semester, Jaxon chiseled away at many of the hard layers BJ had in his life. BJ still regularly gave Jaxon a tough time about not hooking up with girls, not drinking with him, and not doing other things a lot of the high school boys were getting involved with. They were developing a good friendship but were still nothing alike in their beliefs or actions.

It was the last week of the school year, and Jaxon felt confident that BJ would turn him down, but he stayed with his weekly routine of asking BJ whether he wanted to join him at FCA that week. He said, "Hey, man! Last week of FCA. You in?"

He was getting ready to move right along to the next subject, when BJ surprised him by saying, "We'll see."

Jaxon quickly turned his head back toward BJ. His eyebrows were raised almost to the ceiling at this new response. BJ didn't commit, but he didn't decline the offer. As far as Jaxon was concerned, this was progress, and he was excited about the new answer. He didn't think BJ would show up, but he was excited about the possibility of him at least considering going.

To Jaxon's and everyone else's surprise, BJ made an appearance at the last Fellowship of Christian Athletes meeting of the school year.

BJ walked inside the gym and the first person he saw was one of his favorite teachers.

Mr. Walker walked up to BJ and reached to shake his hand. "Look who's here. I'm glad to see you've joined us this morning. I'm surprised, but I'm happy about it."

BJ extended his hand to Mr. Walker. "Good morning Mr. Walker. Sorry, this is my first time. I've been aggravated about this all year by Jaxon, so I figured I'd check it out. What do I have to do?"

"Nothing. You don't have to do anything. Feel free to engage and interact with your friends. When we get started, I'll do most of the talking and we may have a few students say some prayers for us. How's that sound to you?"

BJ was just as surprised as everyone else. He had no idea so many of the other kids from school would be there. There were students representing all the other sports, not just football. He had always just assumed it was some kind of boring Bible study and had never even asked what it was about. He didn't expect to see guys and girls there either. There were a lot of people there he never knew were even involved. Jaxon was the only person he ever even heard talk about FCA. BJ barely said a word, other than greeting people as he arrived, because he felt like an outsider among a group of athletes he'd ruled over for so long.

# 11
## Iron Sharpens Iron

All the defensive players are still on the field, waiting to see what is going to happen with Jaxon. Everyone is kneeling by now except Phoenix. Phoenix is still standing cautiously, close to his best friend.

Phoenix Horne is the middle linebacker on the team and as tough as nails. He is the roughest guy on the team, and most of the college football world is afraid of him, including most of his own teammates. He takes no mercy on any ball carrier or quarterback, and he takes pride in knocking people out of games. He does not believe in God and has no desire to kneel and pray to someone who will allow his friend to get hurt like this.

Phoenix is the cocaptain of the defense, an All-Southeastern Conference selection, All-American, and a can't-miss, first-round draft pick. He may possibly be the second player taken in the draft, selected only behind his best friend. Phoenix is also Jaxon's roommate. These two star athletes are the most competitive and amazingly gifted players the EMU Angels have ever seen.

As Phoenix watches over his fallen brother, he thinks back to the day they met.

It had been their first day on campus together. They had both been told to arrive on campus ahead of the other students, because as football players, they had to begin preparations for the upcoming season. They were incoming freshmen and two of the most highly recruited prospects in the country. It was an amazing feat to land both of these young stars on the same team.

You wouldn't know it from their relationship now, but it wasn't an instant friendship between them. Because both of these young future stars were extremely competitive, they were battling hard to earn starting positions on the team. Both players were considered the best of the freshman class, but they were going up against nearly grown men at this point. They were going to have to work tremendously hard to prove they belonged on the field at such young ages and were worthy of all the hype.

They pushed each other and challenged each other on every conditioning drill. During the one-mile run the whole team had to do, they sprinted to the very end, finishing neck and neck. During all their forty-yard dash drills, they traded outrunning one another regularly, but nobody ran harder than either of these two. They ran through the cone drills as smoothly as a sports car on a racetrack. They both were out to prove they were better than the other and everyone else on the team.

They played different positions, but neither player would accept that the other person was more talented. It was a competitive spirit the coaches drooled over. With these two pushing each other the way they did, they made the entire team work harder just to try to keep up.

They fought and battled with one another the entire summer during workouts and practices. As hard as they worked on the field, they worked even harder in the weight room. Before they even got to play in a game, just by watching these guys work out, the coaches were certain they would go pro as soon as they were eligible.

On the field and in the weight room, these two players were nearly identical in the way they performed. Off the field, however, they were as different as night and day. Jaxon came from a great home, with hard-working parents, where Christian values had been instilled in him from the very beginning. Phoenix came from a broken and abusive home. His mom had died from a drug overdose, and his dad was in prison for murder. He had been raised by his older brother, the leader of a major gang.

Phoenix's gods were violence and hard work. He had discovered at a young age that if he wanted something, he had to go and take it, because nobody was going to give it to him. His brother, King, was a rough character, but he always pushed Phoenix to become something better than himself. King said Phoenix was a gifted athlete and did his best to coach him throughout his high school years. King also tried shielding Phoenix from a lot of the crime committed by himself and his fellow gang members. At the end of the day, Phoenix's family was a bunch of hardened gang members and criminals. That was the life he knew.

The entire gang knew that if Phoenix was to get mixed up in any trouble, with or without any member of the gang being involved, they would all have to answer to King. They all watched out for him and did their best to safeguard him from their world.

Phoenix's experiences in college were much different from Jaxon's. Phoenix was focused on playing football, working out, and having physical relationships with every girl he could. He had no loyalty to anyone but himself. He believed the only thing college was good for was a mandatory avenue before going to the National Football League. It was a necessary evil. He figured that since he was required to put in at least two years of college ball before going pro, he might as well make it as fun as possible.

Jaxon and Phoenix spent the entire summer getting ready for the season and learning more about one another. In a lot of ways, Phoenix reminded Jaxon of BJ. He knew Phoenix was a natural leader and was a great man underneath a mountain of arrogance and toughness. He was aware of Phoenix's lifestyle and priorities, but that didn't deter him from the investment he was ready to make in Phoenix's life. He believed there was a lot more to Phoenix than he himself was yet aware of. Jaxon believed God had gifted Phoenix with the skills and work ethic he had not just to be a great athlete but also to make a difference in this world. Phoenix's goal was to go to the National Football League, and Jaxon had set his goal as well. His new goal was to lead Phoenix to Christ.

Phoenix and Jaxon had both been randomly assigned different roommates when they arrived on campus, but Jaxon had a different plan. He believed that because they were both such high-profile recruits, and they were both dominating at practice, the coaches would be willing to entertain a new idea.

Jaxon went to his defensive coordinator and asked, "Coach, since you're over roommate assignments, do you mind changing things up and putting me in with Phoenix Horne?"

"Why should I do that? It takes a lot of time to change those assignments. There is a lot of work that goes into that."

Jaxon wasn't sure the coach would go for his main reason of wanting to switch, which was to witness to Phoenix on a regular basis, so he shared with him his alternate reason. "Coach, I have always worked my tail off to be the best I can be. But I've got to tell ya, I've never had anyone push me to work harder than Phoenix does. That guy is a beast. With the way he pushes me and makes our team better, I want to be around him as much as possible. Besides, if I am able to build a stronger relationship with him, I am hopeful I'll be able to convince him to stay here through graduation."

Even though Jaxon had a deeper plan, those statements were true, and the coach wasn't about to pass up an opportunity to keep either of these guys until they graduated. He and the other coaches had already gotten their minds right about losing these guys early to the NFL, and the coach was ecstatic about the possibility of having this duo on his team for four seasons. Before he even responded to Jaxon, he already envisioned holding the numerous national championship trophies he believed they could win.

The coach stood there for a moment, reached to shake Jaxon's hand and said, "Let me talk to Phoenix. He should be in here any minute. You move along and I'll let you know."

Phoenix walked into the room and the coach motioned him over.

"What up, Coach?"

The coach figured he would try the same thing on Phoenix that Jaxon had tried on him. "Phoenix, we've all been impressed with you. There was a lot of hype around you and I've gotta tell ya, you're the real deal."

"Thanks, Coach."

"I need your help though. This Jaxon kid has a lot of potential. I really want to partner him up with someone that can push him and make him great. Since you're both freshmen, I was hoping you would be his roommate so you could motivate him to work hard and get us ready to compete for national titles. What do you think?"

Phoenix paused and thought for a moment. He stepped away from the coach and then right back toward him. "Coach, I see what you're sayin. To tell you the truth, I don't care a thing in the world about that boy gettin' any better. But I do want to win. If he plays well, our team plays well. If our team plays well, we win more games. The more games we win, the more recognition I get from NFL scouts and that will help my draft status. Count me in."

Phoenix and Jaxon got along great as roommates. Jaxon was clean, organized, and very considerate as a roommate. Phoenix, on the other hand, liked to have a good time, which was very different from Jaxon's idea of a good time and was a slob around the apartment. Phoenix was an all-in kind of guy. He worked out as hard as Jaxon and partied on a level all his own. They were extremely different from one another socially and spiritually, but they had a mutual respect for each other's talents and work ethic. On the field and in the weight room, they had no equals.

Over time Jaxon and Phoenix became more than great teammates; they also became great friends. Jaxon was patient with Phoenix as a roommate, because he knew that living together would give him the best opportunity to regularly witness to him. More importantly, Jaxon wanted to have full-time access to try to lead Phoenix to Christ. Phoenix made it clear that he wouldn't be converted. Jaxon and Phoenix always had good attitudes about it, and neither of them ever got upset with the other about Jaxon's attempts to lead Phoenix to Christ. Jaxon made verbal comments about Christ regularly, but the way he lived was a far more constant witness about who he believed Christ to be.

Jaxon regularly invited Phoenix to FCA, and Phoenix typically asked, "Are there any hot girls there?" Jaxon just laughed and told Phoenix he would have to go and find out for himself. Phoenix never went, but Jaxon wouldn't hassle him about turning down the constant invitations.

Jaxon went to parties with Phoenix regularly, but he wasn't a drinker, so Phoenix always offered to drink Jaxon's share of alcohol.

Because Phoenix was so big, he could really knock a dent in the alcohol supply at any party. Jaxon always enjoyed going to the parties, because he loved getting to interact with so many people. Even when he was tired or beat up from football, he always made the effort to go, because he knew there were so many witnessing opportunities at every social event on or off campus. They were two of the most popular guys on campus, and as their first season rolled along, their popularity grew with each game.

Their fame soared after a major conference game during their freshman year, in which Jaxon accidentally came up with their new slogan. Jaxon was blindsided on a play, and Phoenix came over to aggressively defend his teammate. At defensive end, Jaxon was pursing the quarterback from around the edge, and he tackled him just as the ball was thrown away. It was a legal play, but one of the offensive lineman was upset about Jaxon taking his quarterback to the ground. As Jaxon stood back to his feet after the play, the lineman violently knocked him back down. Phoenix was in the middle of the field when this happened, and he sprinted to Jaxon's defense. He hit the lineman so hard, his helmet flew off his head as he went flailing to the ground. Phoenix was immediately penalized for unsportsmanlike conduct and nearly thrown out of the game.

After the game, when the reporters asked Jaxon how he felt about Phoenix fighting his battles for him, he just smiled and said, "Well, I guess if you mess with the Bull, you're gonna get the Horne." All the reporters erupted in laughter. Everyone started writing and tweeting the phrase and desperately tried to be the first to get the quote out to the world. It seemed that comment ran 24-7 on every major sports network over the next several weeks.

That phrase was used the rest of the time they were in college. Sports fans, reporters, or sports anchors rarely talked about one and didn't mention the other. There were numerous nicknames for the two stars, and they typically went together. Commonly used nicknames for the duo were phrases such as "Thunder and Lightning," "Salt and Pepper," "Crash and Burn," and so forth. When some sportscaster referred to the two athletes by paired nicknames, they always joked about which was which. They didn't care as long as they were playing well and winning.

Regularly, reporters asked the two teammates about one another, and Phoenix regularly said, "Jaxon may be an amazing Bull, but I am the G.O.A.T. That stands for the 'greatest of all time,' for all you novices out there." Jaxon constantly referred to Phoenix as "Goat." Phoenix was never short on confidence or cockiness.

At the end of their first season, things started to get even more competitive. Both players ended their freshman season while being named the best players in the entire country at their respective positions. Phoenix was the award winner for the best linebacker in the country, and Jaxon won the award as the best defensive end in the country. Both of these accomplishments were amazing for freshmen to be able to win, especially considering they were on the same team.

Where the competition really got ramped up was when Jaxon became the first defensive end to ever win the Heisman Trophy. Because that trophy goes to the best college football player in the nation, Phoenix set his sights on it as well. Jaxon was a more versatile player, and because of his speed, size, and athleticism, he was able to be used in a variety of ways on the field.

There was always a healthy level of competition between the two of them, but because of their ferociousness, there were several times when people thought they were upset with each other and were about to fight. They came across as angry during their workouts, when in reality they were on fire for perfection. If one saw the other slack off one bit, he jumped on the other guy like a junkyard dog. It was amazing how much they fed off each other and made each other better. There was always a level of respect when it came to receiving the stern feedback, no matter how roughly it was delivered.

Phoenix always joked about how they looked out for one another as roommates. He said that because he didn't like to go to class; Jaxon was great at encouraging him to go every day. To return the good favor, Phoenix regularly brought two girls home at the same time and always told Jaxon he had selflessly brought one back for him.

Every girl Phoenix ever brought over became overwhelmingly excited about the possibility of getting to spend some quality time with Jaxon. Even though he had the well-known reputation as someone who wouldn't hook up, there was always hope that Jaxon would change his mind. The second of the two girls Phoenix brought over typically hung out in the living room with Jaxon. More often than not, Jaxon would have them visiting his church within the next two Sundays. He just had such a charisma about him that it was difficult for people to turn down his invitations. The local pastor loved having Jaxon attend his church for many reasons, but he credited their large increase in attendance to Jaxon's ability to lure students to early Sunday mornings.

# 12
## Change of Plan

Phoenix continues pacing back and forth on the field, just steps away from Jaxon. He feels like a chained beast, waiting to be turned loose. Everyone else is still and quiet, but Phoenix is anxious and angry. He continues staring down at Jaxon with all the trainers and medical staff now surrounding him, ready for his brother to get up and get going. His adrenalin is still pumping trough his veins like a racehorse on race day. He is jacked and primed for action.

"Hold on, JB," Fish is telling his fallen buddy. "We are going to take care of you. Hang in there. We've got you." Fish is getting nervous too but is trying to keep it together for Jaxon's sake.

The adrenaline running through Phoenix's system was a feeling he loved and worked hard to recreate as often as he could. Individually, in high school and during their first year of college, he and Jaxon had been known for their unmatched work ethic and their unbelievable workouts.

After their freshman season was over, they decided to take things to the next level. They performed insane workout routines together; this fact caused the strength coaches to have to regularly explain that they weren't the ones assigning the crazy workouts. Due to onlookers and social media, their workouts were no secrets to the world. The coaches were constantly having to defend themselves, because they were afraid they would be accused of injuring one of the stars.

In addition to their regularly scheduled workouts with the team, Phoenix and Jaxon could be seen all over campus and town, working out as if their lives were on the line. Weekly for up to three hours at a time, they took turns pushing and pulling large vehicles. To make things more difficult, they didn't push them on a smooth road; they pushed them through overgrown fields.

There was an old mom-and-pop sawmill just outside of town, where they chopped firewood, which was delivered to stores and homes around town. They used the handsaws to cut large logs into smaller logs, and they carried large logs around the lumberyard to build strength. When they finished, actual sawmill workers used professional machinery to move the heavy lumber.

Because other students knew Phoenix and Jaxon spent a lot of time doing conditioning drills on the school's intramural fields, eager students were always out there, trying their best to give the studs some competition. There was an unwritten rule that they didn't try to talk to them or get in their way, but other students were a constant source of inspiration for Jaxon and Phoenix.

Students lined up beside the finely tuned athletes, eager to run sprints with them. Phoenix and Jaxon were always focused on their own routine and never waited for the other students to get ready, but there was always a "Who's next?" kind of theme when those two ran. As soon as one sprint was over, there was another person next in line, ready to make a memory.

There seemed to be an endless supply of students ready to challenge

Phoenix and Jaxon on their speed training. Jaxon or Phoenix always won all the drills early in the workouts, but as the conditioning routine continued for the duration of the workouts, fresher runners on occasion won. This motivated Jaxon and Phoenix to work even harder, because they didn't like the idea of another student on campus bragging about outrunning them. It didn't matter that Jaxon and Phoenix were two hours into a workout and that the student who beat them had been there less than ten minutes. Jaxon and Phoenix knew that if they lost to a regular student, the video would go viral, and everyone across the country would wonder who the new, unknown speedster in the clip was.

Over the course of the next few years of living, playing, and training together, Jaxon and Phoenix had become inseparable. It didn't seem to matter how different they were outside of sports; they had an undeniable and unshakable bond. They were two of the most talked about, scrutinized, sought after, and amazing athletes in the country. Everyone seemed to want to have a part in their story.

They were both to be feared on the field, but Jaxon had a gentlemanly spirit about knocking someone's head off. He would hit someone so hard and fast that he would think he had been hit by a jumbo jet. Afterward, he quickly helped the person to his feet and said things like, "God bless you," "Hang in there," or some other form of encouragement after each unpleasant encounter.

Phoenix, on the other hand, wanted someone not only to fear him but also to dislike him. He wanted to make certain the person never wanted to see him again play after play. He hit the person just as hard as Jaxon, but he would step on the person's face or talk about his momma before he considered even a positive word of encouragement. Phoenix had the reputation as a reckless, headhunting, and dangerous quarterback killer. Jaxon was considered an unshakable, cool, calm, and collected assassin on the field.

It was late in their junior season when his teammates finally saw Jaxon wasn't perfect. They were in the middle of practice when the offensive tackle on his side of the ball slammed him to the ground. The lineman was doing his job, trying to protect his quarterback from the pursuing Jaxon. As Jaxon was trying to get around him, he lost his footing, and his teammate hurled him to the ground. Jaxon hit the ground tremendously hard and got up fighting mad. As he jumped to his feet and punched the unsuspecting lineman in the helmet, he angrily yelled at his teammate for everyone on the field to hear. He stopped himself before he finished the insulting sentence, but the damage had already been done with the punch.

It was as if the whole world stopped in its tracks. Everyone on the field went silent and was completely stunned by what had happened. Nobody had ever seen Jaxon lose his cool before. The first one to break the silence was Phoenix.

He yelled out, "I'll finish that fight and that sentence for you. You mess with the Bull, and you get the Horne, baby!"

Everyone started laughing at Phoenix's response to the awkward silence on the field. Everyone except Jaxon. He walked back to his side of the ball with his head down and his temper up.

Jaxon was embarrassed and ashamed for losing his temper, especially toward one of his friends and teammates. He didn't say a word. He was extremely upset. He was mad that he had gotten beat but even madder at himself for the way he had reacted. He would have quickly forgiven anyone on the field for doing the exact same thing, but he felt he had an obligation to those guys to set a better example.

He knew he owed it to Jesus to represent Him with the utmost integrity and felt as if he had failed.

Phoenix couldn't have been more excited. He ran over to Jaxon, threw his arm around him, and playfully said, with excitement in his voice, "Finally! Look who finally got savage! I didn't think you had it in ya. Who we gonna hit next? Let's cuss some people out. This is gonna be awesome. Let it out, Bull. You been holdin that in too long."

During the rest of the year, Phoenix had a lot of fun with that incident. He said things to people like, "You better not make my boy mad! If you get him mad, he will go Hulk on you. He will punch you and cuss out yo momma."

It took a while before Jaxon could laugh about the funny stuff Phoenix said, but it was difficult at first. Phoenix couldn't figure it out. Phoenix punched people and cussed people out all the time in practice. He figured that was just part of the game, and then he could get on about his business.

That night after practice, Jaxon asked Phoenix to meet him in their living room. After they both got settled, Jaxon said to Phoenix, "You are my brother on and off the field, and I owe you more than what I gave you today."

Phoenix didn't have a clue what Jaxon was talking about and said, "What did you give me, and where is the rest of it?"

"I'm serious. I'm talking about my behavior on the field today. I let you down, and I'm asking you to forgive me."

Phoenix quickly responded with the wave of his hand as he turned his head. "Psshhhh! Bruh, get outta here with that. That junk was funny. I'm glad you did it. Everyone was glad you did it. Except ol big'un that you punched. That was funny. If you're gonna apologize to someone, it probably should be him. Forget it. That ain't nothin, dawg!"

"It was something to me. I have been the best example I can be

105

for you the whole time we've known each other. I try to demonstrate something to you I want you to have in your life. I have tried my best to show you a Christlike example ever since we met, and today wasn't that example. You are a great accountability partner, and you don't even realize how.

"My first priority isn't to be in the NFL, but that is a high one. Above all else, I want to serve my God to the best of my ability. I want everyone to come to know and love God as I do. I want everyone to experience a life in heaven with Jesus. I want to be known as a godly man, not just as a great ballplayer."

Phoenix assured him, "Bruh, I know all that. We been living together all this time. Trust me, I know. Everyone knows. You're the best dude any of us know or ever met. What you did today ain't gonna change that. I'm acting like I know that stuff you been preachin' all this time better than you. Believe it or not, all that holy mess you tell everyone, I hear some of it too. You thought you were gonna be some kind of Reggie White on the field, but I bet ol Reggie did some damage in his day. You know what? Maybe I need to be a preacher."

Jaxon couldn't help but laugh about Phoenix's version of encouragement, but he wasn't letting himself completely off the hook. He told Phoenix, "You are my brother, no matter what. I will always be your brother. You know how I feel about this, because we have talked about it many times before. What I want most for you is for you to know Jesus. You know I want you in heaven with me, bruh. I have never pressured you about it, but I have always done my best to be a good example. I don't wanna let you or anyone else down. You know?"

Phoenix stood up, grabbed a football, and started tossing it from one hand to the other. "Bruh, we talked about this before. You know I don't believe in that stuff. You know I drink, I cuss, I fight. And for the life of me, I don't understand you not gettin with all these girls that want you. One thing I do know is that you love that God of yours. I don't know what He's done to convince you He's real, but if He does that for me, I'm all in. I promise! And I'll give you all the credit."

Jaxon started laughing and then paused before he spoke. "I'm serious, bruh. I don't want the credit. You give it to the One who deserves it." As he pointed to heaven. "Since you seem like you'd now be open to it, what would it take to convince you He's real?"

Because it was their junior season, they were both eligible to go pro. Because of Jaxon's accomplishments and versatility, there was no doubt in anyone's mind that he would be the first pick in the draft, regardless of the needs of the team who received the first pick. Phoenix was a definite first rounder, but he was predicted to go in the middle of the first round to a few different potential teams in need of a linebacker.

Phoenix thought for a moment and sarcastically dropped to his knees, raising his hands toward the sky as he said, "If I go ahead of you in the draft, that will prove to me that God exists. I will drop to my knees at that very moment and give my life to your God." He started laughing as he playfully looked toward the sky. He then lowered his arms and continued tossing the football from one hand to the other as he looked back at Jaxon with a devious smile.

"Done!" Jaxon said with lots of confidence.

"How's that?" Phoenix replied. Jaxon knew Phoenix was ready to go pro and was planning to leave school early. "Based on everything that every single draft expert, coach, fan, or idiot with an opinion says, there ain't no way I'm going ahead of you. Nobody is."

Phoenix was very confident in his skills, but he knew a team would pick him based on their need at the linebacker position. He also knew any team would pick Jaxon because he would be a valuable bargaining chip for trades because he would be the best player in the draft. Any team that drafted Jaxon would more than likely keep him, because they could use him just about anywhere on the field.

Jaxon said, "You're entering the draft. I'm not going to. You'll definitely go way ahead of me if you go this year and I go next year. You'll beat me by a whole year."

"What are you talking about? You ain't going pro this year?" Phoenix aggressively asked as he climbed back to his feet. "We're going pro together. That's what we been dreaming about. Don't mess this up."

"I know. We have. I've been praying about it and giving it a lot of thought, but I have more to do here. I ain't done yet. I started here, and I'm gonna finish here. I believe God is doing some amazing things here, and He's got something big planned before I leave. I don't know what it is, but I can feel it."

Phoenix, voicing his frustrations, began quickly and repeatedly pointing at his own head. "Bruh, I ain't believing this. You need to get your mind right."

Phoenix started walking away from Jaxon and sharply spun back around as he loudly continued, "You gotta think about your future. You gonna be the first pick. You don't wait for next year, when you're the first pick. You could be throwin' away millions. You ain't movin' up from the first pick. It don't get no better than that."

Jaxon just flashed his big smile. "You'll see."

Phoenix was clearly frustrated with his friend and roommate. "I'm going to bed. You need to sleep on this, and you'll be thinking straight tomorrow. This ain't right! We are both going pro this year. We are sticking to the plan and going to the league together. You'll be straight in the morning."

# 13
## Where You Go, I Go

Fish is starting to get fidgety. He is ready to see some sort of movement from Jaxon or hear his voice. So far, the only life he has seen from him is a slight smile and erratic movements of his eyes. He is looking around at what the professional trainers are doing, and he repeatedly looks back down at Jaxon's eyes.

Fish can't believe Jaxon is in this situation. As he anxiously waits for whatever happens next, he thinks to himself how fortunate he is to be with his friend at this moment. He remembers that he would not be in this situation if it were not for Jaxon, not because of this particular injury to Jaxon but because of the injuries to Jaxon and BJ while they were in high school.

While in high school, the first time Jaxon was thought to be knocked out and Fish smacked him on the head a few times, trying to wake him up, the school's athletic trainer had decided to educate Fish on more than just running water out to the thirsty players. He continued to be the football manager, but he became much more educated about what to do and, more importantly, what not to do to injured players.

After BJ's injury, Andy went with Jaxon nearly every time he visited BJ. Where Andy really became intrigued was at physical therapy. He became fascinated with the idea of helping athletes return from injuries. Jaxon encouraged Fish to watch, ask questions, and learn as much as he could from the athletic trainers and physical therapist they had as resources in high school. Jaxon knew that even though Fish was fast, Fish had little chance of participating as one of his teammates in football.

Jaxon was always a great encourager of everyone but especially Fish. They were great friends growing up, but he knew that as college approached, he would have to find another way for Fish to be part of the experience with him. He knew that even though Fish had come a long way in his faith, he believed Fish would be easily led astray in college if he didn't establish healthy friendships and habits. Jaxon had always been strong in his stance on things he didn't want in his life, but Fish was desperate to be part of a group. So far, Fish believed the only reason people tolerated him was because he was such close friends with Jaxon. Fish was certain that if Jaxon weren't around, nobody would want him around.

With Andy spending so much time listening to Jaxon witness to people, especially to BJ during their freshman year, he developed a much better understanding of the gospel and a deeper desire to develop his own relationship with Christ. During their remaining years in high school, Fish in many ways developed a lot as a young man. Even though he was always quiet, he developed a stronger sense of belonging and gained a lot of confidence. He felt extremely useful and developed a sense of belonging as a manager of the football team. He loved being part of the action.

Jaxon could tell how attentive Andy was when they went to the hospital to visit people. He noticed how focused Andy became during physical therapy visits and how he rarely left the athletic trainer's side during football games. He was convinced that Fish would make a great athletic trainer and that this could possibly be his ticket to keeping his friend with him wherever he played college ball.

Midway through their senior year in high school, Jaxon approached Andy with his idea. "Hey Fish, I know we've talked about it before, but have you really decided where you're gonna go to college? I mean, like, for real gonna go?"

Fish looked at him with a confused expression. "I'm going wherever you go." He said it as if there was never a doubt.

"Yeah, but I still don't know where I'm gonna go. Not for sure. These recruiting trips are getting kind of crazy, and I wanna be able to make a difference wherever I go. What if I pick a school you don't wanna go to?"

"What do you mean?" Fish asked. Before Jaxon could respond, Fish continued, "You're not gonna go to the West Coast, are you? Please don't say Hawaii. It looks cool and all, but I don't know if I could handle it if you go that far away. We said we would talk about it before either of us picked."

Jaxon just started laughing and responded with, "No. I ain't decided nothing yet. Besides, if I do go to Hawaii, you'd have plenty of reasons to come and visit."

"What are we talking about then?"

Jaxon then laid out his master plan. "Why don't you be a trainer?"

Andy followed up Jaxon's question with one of his own. "What do you mean? Like, an athletic trainer?"

"Yeah. Why not?"

"Because I'm the manager. I'm good at being a manager."

Jaxon agreed. "You're awesome at it. The best. I'm just thinking you really love all that health stuff. I see how you get about the injuries and stuff. I think you'd be good at it. Besides, I need someone to help me when I get hurt. Someone I trust."

"You ain't hurt. You don't get hurt. I'd be bored."

Jaxon reassured him, "Yeah, but if I do get hurt, I need you. You know me better than anyone. You can learn how I like my tape done, help me with my treatments after practice and games, and keep me running on all cylinders."

Andy started getting nervous, because it was something new, and new always overwhelmed him. "I don't know how to do that stuff. I'm a manager. I know how to do that. I'm good at that."

Jaxon reassured him, "You could learn. You're smart, and you pick stuff up real fast. You'd be awesome at it. Besides, if you're a trainer, you could go anywhere I go."

"What do you mean? How?"

"All these school visits I go on, I see student trainers everywhere the players are. At some schools, it seems the trainers are more involved with the players than the coaches. I ain't been on a single visit where I have met any managers except their head manager. No student managers, though."

Andy, trying to defend his position, said, "That's because the managers work behind the scenes. That's where I like to be. I don't need the attention. I don't want the attention. You know I ain't like you. You're good at getting the attention." Andy paused for a moment, dropped his head, and seemed almost embarrassed to admit it as he shyly said, "I don't like attention."

"I get it," Jaxon said as he put his hand on Andy's shoulder. "I really do. I don't want you to think of it as getting attention." Jaxon leaned in and put his other hand on Andy's other shoulder as he continued, "Just think of the witnessing you'll get to do."

"What do you mean?" Andy asked as if that was his automatic response to anything Jaxon said.

"Just think how much one-on-one time you'll get to spend with the players. If they are hurt, need to be taped up, or are rehabbing, you'll get a ton of time with them. You'll be able to know their hearts and learn what they like and dislike. It could be awesome. You'll develop better relationships with them than anyone else."

"I don't know. I ain't good at that stuff like you are. You can talk to anybody. I don't like it," Andy said, still trying to avoid this idea of Jaxon's.

Jaxon reminded him of the mission trips they went on together with the Bull family. "Brother, you did awesome when we went on all those mission trips. You connect with people," Jaxon said as he stood tall and held his arms out wide. "People trust you and aren't afraid to tell you things. People just wanna play ball with me, but they want you to really know them. You're the best listener I've ever met."

"You mean I don't talk," Andy fired back at Jaxon.

"People who don't talk make much better listeners than people who never shut up," Jaxon said, reinforcing his point. "Who are you gonna trust more—people who know nothing about you or people who know everything about you because they listen to you? If people trust you, they will listen to you about Jesus. I can't think of anything better."

Andy sat there for a moment and contemplated what Jaxon was saying. Jaxon could tell Andy was uncomfortable with the idea of exploring an area he wasn't familiar with, but he was always impressed by how Jaxon connected with people about Jesus. He wasn't as strong of a believer as Jaxon, but he was impressed with Jaxon's faith.

"I don't even know how to get started. What would I need to do?" Andy sheepishly asked.

Jaxon became excited about Andy's opening up to the idea. "I'll tell you what. How about you come along with me on my next recruiting trip? I've got a big one next weekend, and they'll let me take whoever I want to go with me. While I'm talking to coaches, you can talk to the athletic trainers. You can get a feel for it, just like I'm trying to get a feel for things. How's that sound?"

"I've never been recruited. I don't know what to do. What am I supposed to do?"

"You don't do anything," Jaxon said as he flung his arms across one another as if he were calling a base runner safe. "They do everything!" Jaxon continued with excitement. "You just show up and do whatever they have for you to do. It's cool. They give you stuff, feed you, take you to fun things and ball games, and show you everything on campus."

The next weekend came around, and Jaxon and Andy were on their way to a smaller college program. The college was in the process of trying to lure Jaxon to campus. "Just be yourself," Jaxon told Andy as he was trying to get him to relax. "When we get there, you just let them tell you everything you need to know. It's really easy, and you don't even have to talk if you don't want to."

With Jaxon being one of the top recruits in the country, he had plenty of schools to choose from. Every school that convinced him to go to campus for a recruiting trip rolled out the red carpet for him. He was primarily interested in playing for one of the major programs, but he wanted to go on this recruiting trip because, even though it was a smaller school, they had a great athletic training program. He figured Andy would be able to learn a lot on this visit and be better informed on what he needed to know before going to the other schools in the future. He told the school in advance that he was bringing Andy along with him. Jaxon made it abundantly clear that he wanted them to tell Fish everything he needed to know about their athletic training program.

When they arrived on campus, they went straight to the athletic compound. Andy was in awe of everything he was seeing. He had seen only high school facilities and was amazed by how high tech the facilities were. The team's head athletic trainer came out to meet them and said, "Hey, Bull. We're glad to have you here. We couldn't believe it when they told us you were coming to see us. That's awesome that you're interested in our athletic training program."

"Nice to meet you, sir. Meet my friend, Andy. He wants to be a trainer." Jaxon quickly introduced Andy to the trainer, but the trainer barely even acknowledged Fish. The head trainer did a great job of explaining the program and what all they offered to the athletes. He showed them all the fancy equipment and tried his best to show how well taken care of Jaxon would be if he were to play ball at their school.

Andy was amazed by all he saw. He couldn't believe how much he enjoyed the visit and how great they had treated them. He was excited about getting to learn more about something he had previously witnessed only from a distance.

Jaxon didn't leave the school feeling the same way. He was upset that the trainer had focused only on him and barely even spoke to Fish. He believed he'd made it clear that he wanted the recruiting trip to be about his friend and not him, but the trainer had focused all his efforts on the superstar. Andy was actually relieved nobody had tried to talk to him or ask him any questions. He didn't want any attention, and he thought the trip had been great because he'd been practically invisible.

As they were driving home, Andy said to Jaxon, "That was awesome. Is that the kind of stuff you normally get to do on these trips?"

Jaxon, still somewhat frustrated, said, "That stunk. That one wasn't any good."

"What do you mean? I thought it was awesome. I've never seen anything like that. Their stuff is way better than ours. Even at the doc's office, they don't have anything like that."

"Just wait, bro. We will go to some big-time programs soon. You'll see. Those guys don't know what they are doing. I've seen some schools that blow that one out of the water. You're not gonna believe it, Fish. You'll see."

"I don't know how it could get better than that. That was really cool. I would go—" Andy paused for a moment and thought carefully about his situation.

Jaxon looked over at Andy, waiting for him to finish his thought.

Andy continued. "You know what? I think I might be an athletic trainer. I think it's cool to be able to do that stuff. They do a lot more than ours do at school. I didn't know they did all that."

Jaxon smiled as Andy's attitude started to get better and said, "Right? They get after it in there, don't they? Now you see what I mean? Just think what you could do in that kind of environment."

Andy sat there, quietly letting Jaxon's words sink in for a moment. After a few minutes of silence, Andy simply said, "Thank you." He didn't feel like he could say anything else for fear of starting to cry.

"What are you thanking me for?"

"I wouldn't have even thought about it if you hadn't said anything about it. I never would have even considered it." Andy waited a few moments in silence and finished with, "Thank you for being my friend."

At that moment, Jaxon knew to just be quiet and let Andy think. Both of the young men were completely silent the rest of the way home. They had a lot on their minds, and they used the rest of their time in the car for thought and private reflection.

# 14
## Recruiting Greatness

After Jaxon first went to the ground, Coach Davis, the head coach of the EMU Angels, started preparing for the next play. Because his focus was on preparing for the next snap of the ball, he isn't immediately aware of there being an injured player on the field. When he realizes one of his guys isn't moving, his attention shifts from the game to Jaxon.

He is just standing on the sidelines, waiting to see how the trainers will react to Jaxon once they reach him. He keeps his headset on as he tries to listen carefully for information coming from his colleagues in the booth above. He removes his hat and puts his hands on his hips. Now that the trainers are at the scene, he can tell there is something seriously wrong with Jaxon.

Coach Davis eases out onto the field. He cautiously and methodically places one foot on the ground after the other as he inches away from the sideline. It appears as if he is walking slowly enough to give Jaxon time to pop to his feet before he arrives. The leader of this impressive team walks toward Jaxon with his head down, his eyes locked on Jaxon's position. He is doing his best to appear stoic for his team.

Coach Davis is a big man. He is a retired NFL lineman, and he loves Jaxon like his own son. He is no longer the size he had been when he played in the pros, but he is still a big fella. He is the one who had recruited Jaxon, and they had a connection right from the start. With the name Davis, a lot of the players called him "Coach D," just like Jaxon's dad. Jaxon never called him "Coach D," because there was only one "Coach D" in his world.

Coach Davis has reached Jaxon's location on the field, he doesn't want to interfere with the training staff, but he wants to know the status of his best player. He first approaches Phoenix and says, "Back on up, son. Let them do their jobs. They can handle this." Phoenix doesn't say a word and doesn't leave from where he is pacing. He just continues doing what he is doing but respectfully stays out of the way.

Coach Davis pats Phoenix on the back and turns his attention to the mob of trainers. He inches a little closer to Jaxon. He just stands silently for a few moments, and nobody realizes he is even there. The training staff is so focused on caring for Jaxon that they don't stop to update the coach. Andy is still holding Jaxon's head still, and the lead trainer is holding Jaxon's hand.

Coach Davis can hear the lead trainer speaking to Jaxon. He is on his knees, very close to Jaxon's face. "Can you hear me, Bull? Squeeze my hand if you can hear me. Can you feel my hand?"

This line of questioning makes Coach Davis nervous. He knows that if Jaxon hasn't spoken from the time he went down to the time the coach got out here, Jaxon may be unconscious. He isn't able to see whether Jaxon's eyes are open; he can only hear the interrogation by his head trainer. Regardless of his emotional connection with Jaxon, he still has a responsibility to keep his head in the game; for the sake of the entire team, he backs up for a moment and catches his breath. As he backs up a few steps, he drops his head and thinks back to the first time he laid eyes on Jaxon.

"It's not every day you get one of the best young players in the country in your own backyard." Coach Davis said to his coaching staff as he leaned back in his chair and put his feet on his desk. "I'm gonna go over there and watch that boy from Tish County play this Friday night with my own eyes." It wasn't very common for a head coach of an SEC school to go and watch a high school junior, but Jaxon had been generating a lot of talk among the coaches in the state since early in his sophomore year.

Tishomingo County High School was slated to play against their regular, regional matchup, Pain High School, and both teams were solid squads. Pain High School was in the same town as East Mississippi University, so it was very easy for the coach to get in and out with very little advanced planning. Coach Davis figured this would be a great matchup, and he was very likely going to see some players who would eventually play for the Angels anyway. Even if Jaxon didn't have a great game, the hype about him was worth going to see for himself.

Jaxon impressed Coach Davis before even seeing him play. Just his physical presence alone was remarkable. The first time he saw Jaxon, he was at center field as team captain standing face-to-face with the opposing team's captains. Jaxon looked like a grown man standing with a bunch of boys.

Coach Davis wanted a seriously imposing player on his team. He wanted one whom other teams would find intimidating when he stepped off the bus. Jaxon was one of those guys. He had the dangerous look of a grizzly bear. He was impressive, muscular, majestic, and all around an imposing young man.

After the coin toss, Jaxon took his position at the back of his own end zone. He backed all the way down the field, not taking his eyes off the other end zone. He looked focused and determined.

The ball was kicked extremely deep, so Coach Davis momentarily stopped paying attention. He took the time to sign an autograph for a young kid near him. He wasn't aware of Jaxon's stubbornness of bringing the ball out of the end zone, regardless of where he received the kick. Other teams were aware of this bad habit, but they tried their best not to kick it to him, because of how dangerous he was with the ball in his hands. Pain's kicker was so hyper focused on not kicking it to Jaxon's side of the field that he accidentally kicked it directly to him.

Coach Davis signed the young boy's hat and started walking closer to the fence. He leaned into the fence and quickly checked his cell phone. When he heard the crowd start yelling, it finally dawned on him that he had never heard the whistle. All the fans in the stands were yelling for their boys to stop the Bull from breaking through their line of defenders. It seemed like just a split second had passed, and Jaxon was passing the fifty-yard line.

He was gone! There was no catching him. After he crushed the first few defenders who got in his way, he cruised for the remainder of the kick return. He ended up outrunning everyone to the end zone by more than ten yards. The accomplishment was amazing. High schoolers just shouldn't be able to make plays like that, especially high school juniors.

Because Coach Davis didn't see the whole play unfold, he wasn't overly impressed, but his curiosity was definitely sparked. After Tishomingo County kicked off, Jaxon was now on defense and ready to play. Upon the very first snap of the game, Jaxon took one step toward the outside, and when the opposing offensive lineman fell for the move, Jaxon shot back to the inside with a clear path to the quarterback. Within a split second, he had gotten to the quarterback, crushed him, knocked the ball out of his hands, and recovered the loose ball. Jaxon quickly jumped to his feet, scooped up the ball, and sprinted to the length of the field into the end zone. It was less than one minute into the game, and Jaxon had already scored two touchdowns.

Coach Davis had seen enough. He knew the hype was real. This kid was the real deal. He had never seen anything like this before. He had never seen a single player dominate a game the way Jaxon was able to. He knew that because it wasn't an official visit, he wouldn't be able to interact with Jaxon, so he decided it was time to leave. He knew this eleventh-grader would be the best player in next year's recruiting class. Jaxon showed Coach Davis in less than one minute of actual game time that whoever signed this young man would have a game changer to build a team around.

Coach Davis turned away from the field and started walking away as he pulled out his cell phone to call his head recruiter, Coach Franklin. With one hand holding the phone and the other plugging his ear, he shouted to Coach Franklin, "I found our franchise player! He's right here. This kid is probably the best defensive player in the country, and he's only a junior. Get out to the game and watch this kid play. You're not gonna believe it!"

"I'm already here. I'm watching him now. He is everything we heard and more," Coach Franklin said.

"You're already here? Where are you? Did you see those two touchdowns? You might have missed them they were so fast," Coach Davis shouted with great enthusiasm.

"Two touchdowns? You mean sacks. Nobody has scored yet,"

"No! I mean touchdowns. 'Nobody has scored'? Are you even paying attention?" Coach D said with frustration.

Coach Franklin quickly defended himself. "I think I know the difference between a touchdown and a sack."

Coach D shot back, "He scored after the sack. Pay attention!"

Coach Franklin once again defended his ability to scout a game.

"No, he didn't. I'm looking at the scoreboard right now, and there are zeroes on both sides."

In all the excitement of seeing Jaxon's dominance, he forgot that his recruiter was out of town and watching another player that weekend. Coach Franklin just happened to be watching another stud defender during his junior season on the same night.

"Coach D, what are you talking about? I'm watching this middle linebacker everyone in the country is talking about."

"He's a defensive end, not a linebacker."

It finally occurred to Coach Franklin that they might be referring to two different games and two different players. "Coach, where are you?"

Coach Davis said, "I'm at the game! I told y'all I was going to the game."

Coach Franklin quickly updated his boss. "Coach, you do remember that I left town yesterday to watch this Horne kid, don't you?"

Coach Davis sat there in total silence for a moment before he responded. "Oh yeah! I forgot. You've got to see this kid from Tishomingo County. He's what we need on defense. If he keeps this up, he could transform our team."

Coach Franklin reminded him of what he was doing. "Coach, I'm watching this Horne kid right now, and he's unnatural. He's got strength I've never seen in a kid this young before."

"Well, I'm pretty sure I just finished watching his daddy play, and he's our guy. You need to find out everything there is to know about Jaxon Bull. We need to know what kind of kid we are dealing with."

Over the course of the next year, the coaching staff for the EMU Angels found out exactly what kind of person Jaxon was, and they focused a lot of their efforts into recruiting him. Once recruiting season began, Coach Davis visited the Bull family personally. Tishomingo was only about an hour and a half from Pain, so the coach decided he would make a surprise visit to the Bull residence. He believed that even if there was nobody home, he could get more familiar with the area Jaxon was from to give himself a recruiting advantage.

Coach Davis didn't really have much of a plan other than to arrive in Tishomingo and ask around town about the local star. The first place he stopped was a gas station located in the middle of town. As soon as he stepped inside the crowded convenient store, he heard someone say from behind the counter, "Hey, Coach! You lookin' to take Jaxon back with you?"

"I hope so!" Coach Davis responded. Everyone was well aware of the constant flow of recruiters and coaches in and out of the small town. Everyone also knew by sight or sound exactly who the head coaches were of every SEC team. College football ranks extremely high in these parts, probably third only to God and hunting. It was debatable to which order that list was, depending on when and/or whom you asked.

Coach Davis had a knack with people. He was great at relating to others, and that served him well in the world of recruiting. Instead of starting in on his questions about Jaxon, he asked the local townsfolks about hunting and fishing. "Who got this one?" Coach Davis asked as he pointed at a large buck deer head hanging on the back wall of the town's social-gathering hotspot.

That was all it took for the old-timers to completely forget the coach wasn't there for them. Through several laughs, backslaps, and tall tales, he chatted with everyone who came in and out of the convenient store before he finally asked where Jaxon lived. The store's owner stood up from the dirty, old breakfast table and proudly told the coach where to go as he pointed the direction of the Bulls' home.

"Come on in!" Tim yelled across the house.

Coach Davis was surprised to hear those words coming from inside the house, because he hadn't yet identified himself. He paused for a moment, thinking the residents may have been expecting someone else.

"Door's open! Come on in!" Tim repeated.

Coach Davis turned the doorknob and cautiously pushed the door open. "Hey there! I'm Coach Davis. I'm the head coach for the EMU Angels."

"You better not come in then. We're State fans 'round here. You better get on outta here before I turn my Bulldog loose on ya." Mississippi State was one of the in-state rivals of the Angels, so Tim figured he would try to make Coach Davis a little nervous and have some fun with him.

Amanda quickly chimed in, "Don't listen to him! Come on in. Can I offer you something to drink? How 'bout some sweet tea?"

Coach Davis proceeded into the living room with caution. "Yes, ma'am," he said as he smiled and nodded toward Amanda. "Sweet tea would be perfect."

He was tremendously relieved when the first thing he saw was a picture of the Bull family on the living room wall. Tim was wearing an East Mississippi University hat in the photo. The coach, assuming the patriarch of the family was a bit of a kidder, shot back with his own sense of humor. "You must've lost a bet in that picture." He pointed to the family photo.

"Ahhh, man! I didn't think about that picture being up there." Tim laughed as he realized he wouldn't be able to carry on the joke with all the Angel paraphernalia in their house. As Tim reached for the coach's hand, he said, "Coach, I'm Tim Bull. My friends call me 'Dozer.' This here beautiful lady is my lovely bride, Amanda. She's taken, so don't get any funny ideas. Now, if you need a kicker, she's been practicing,"

Tim jokingly said as he patted his backside, insinuating Amanda had been kicking him.

The coach turned toward Amanda and said, "Yeah, I'm sure she could do it. I believe either of you could give half our team a run for their money. Y'all look like you were quite the sensations in your day. What all did you play?"

Tim liked the coach right away. He was always more than willing to talk about his and Amanda's glory days. Amanda always enjoyed talking about Tim's athletic achievements more than her own, but they were very complimentary of one another.

"Coach, you should have seen this woman back when she played ball," Tim continued. "The first time she first dunked it, I believe she was eight years old. I was there. I saw it. You might not believe it, but she ran a four point two when she was eight months pregnant and eating a bucket of chicken. I'm just lucky that I ran a four point one, or I wouldn't have been able to catch her and talk her into becoming my wife."

Amanda walked over to the coach and reached out to shake his hand as she handed him his glass of tea. "Coach, please don't mind him. He's always like this. You can't take him seriously."

Coach Davis firmly shook Amanda's hand and said, "I wouldn't have it any other way, ma'am. I prefer to do a little cuttin' up myself. People always get too nervous when I'm in their home. I love it when you're loose and can be yourself. It helps me be myself too."

Amanda gave the coach a smile and said, "Well, sir, you're in the right place with my husband. Cuttin' up is what he loves to do."

Tim chimed in again. "Come on, y'all. I can be serious!" While sitting on the couch, Tim leaned forward, interlocked his fingers together, and put his elbows on his knees. He said, "Coach, let's get serious for a moment. I know why you're here, and I'm ready to talk business. I haven't played competitively in a few years, but it's like riding a bike. Where do you need me? You want me at quarterback?" Tim stood to his feet and he began loosening up his arm.

Coach Davis gave a slight laugh. "How much eligibility you got left?"

Amanda picked up her purse, gave Tim a quick kiss on the cheek and gave the coach a wave on her way to the front door. "You boys are gonna have to excuse me. I can see nothing productive is going to come from this today, so I'm gonna get going. Coach, it was nice to meet you. Good luck to ya!"

Coach Davis turned to Tim and said, "I didn't mean to run her off."

Tim responded as he started toward the back door of the house, "Naw. You didn't. She was already leaving when you knocked on the door. She's going down to the hospital. Come on around back." Without question, Coach Davis stood to his feet and followed along. Coach Davis and Tim walked through the house and into the backyard.

"You wanna play twenty-one?" Tim asked Coach Davis as he picked up the basketball and aggressively tossed the ball to the coach. Coach Davis was considered a young head coach and was around the same age as Tim, so Tim was excited about the possibility of someone playing with someone that wasn't half his age.

Tim said, "You look like you can play. I don't get to play many folks my age. At least ones that are still able to move without pulling, tearing, or breaking something. I'm used to having to play with Jaxon and all his buddies. They wear this old man out."

Coach Davis was very surprised and excited to have the opportunity to play backyard basketball. "You know what? I'd love to. Let me change shoes, and I'll be right back." The coach ran out to his truck, put on some basketball shoes from his gym bag, and ran back around the house. He was acting like a kid who was about to get to do something he wasn't normally allowed to do.

"Win by two?" Coach Davis asked as he rounded the corner.

For the next hour, Coach Davis and Tim played multiple games of twenty-one. They were both sweating, laughing, and having a great time together. There were talking trash to each other and acting like old buddies who had known each other for years. Not one time during his entire visit with the Bull family did Jaxon's name ever come up about recruiting. Coach Davis never even mentioned Jaxon.

After they finished playing basketball, Coach Davis said to Tim, "Mr. Bull, I haven't had this much fun in quite a while. It's not very often I can just be one of the guys. Everywhere I go, I have to be 'the head coach.' Getting to play ball with you has been exactly what I needed."

"Well, Coach, you're welcome to come back here for another whoopin' anytime you need to feel normal. That 'Mr. Bull' business isn't welcome here though. After seeing you play ball the way you do, you've earned the right to call me 'Dozer.'"

Coach Davis was very impressed with how well Tim had handled himself on the basketball court. "All right then, Dozer. Man, you sure can shoot. I don't consider this a legit win, though. I know you've got home court advantage down here, so you'll have to come over to Pain and play on *my* court sometime. We've gotta even the playing field. You made so many shots. I feel like you invited me around here just to rebound for you."

Tim smiled and winked at the coach. "Well, I guess I got lucky today."

Tim walked Coach Davis back around to his vehicle and gave him a bottle of water to take with him as he drove back to Pain. Tim and Coach Davis shook hands and exchanged pleasantries before they parted ways.

Later that evening, Amanda got home about five minutes after Jaxon. Amanda opened the front door and saw Tim and Jaxon sitting in the living room, watching television. She walked in, shutting the door behind her. She stood there for a moment and waited for a reaction from her two favorite fellas.

After standing there silently for about ten seconds, she finally threw up her hands and said, "Well?"

"Oh! Hey, Mom!" Jaxon said enthusiastically, believing she was waiting on a greeting.

"Don't just 'Hey, Mom' me!" Amanda exclaimed as she walked farther into the house and dropped her purse on the living room table.

Jaxon, not sure what to do, asked, "What?"

Amanda quickly followed with, "Well, what did Coach Davis have to say?"

Jaxon was confused and couldn't tell whether she was talking to him or Tim at this point. He responded the way most teenagers do when asked a question by a parent. "Huh?"

Now, taking off her shoes as she sat down on the couch beside Tim, Amanda asked, "Coach Davis. What did he have to say? Was it a good visit?"

Tim remained quiet and just sat there like he was in trouble. Jaxon inquisitively asked, "Visit? East Mississippi's Coach Davis? Coach Davis wants me to come for a visit? Really? Where did you hear that?"

Amanda was a little confused at this point and asked, "Did you not see him? Timothy, have you not talked to your son about seeing him?"

"What are y'all talking about?" Jaxon asked. "See who?"

Tim leaned back into the couch and said, "Oh? Did I forget to mention that?"

"Mention what?" Jaxon asked. "Y'all got me so confused right now."

Amanda chimed in again. "Coach Davis came by the house today. Tim, why didn't you tell him? What did he have to say about Jaxon?"

Tim stood up and puffed out his chest a little bit. "Who says he said anything about Jaxon?" He walked over to straighten up a picture on the wall, leaned back to see if it was straight, and then paused for a dramatic effect as he let out a big breath of air. "As it happens, we played basketball for about an hour, and he asked me to come to Pain to play ball?"

"You?" Jaxon said with a lot of surprise and a little bit of laughter in his voice. "What kind of ball does he want you to play? Pickleball? Bocce ball? He does know you're like eighty, right?"

Tim, defending his honor, said, "Boy, I can still whip your tail out back. Ain't nobody around here can shoot like your old man. As it happens, I put a whoopin' on that feller in an hour's worth of twenty-one."

"Yeah, right!" came from Amanda and Jaxon at the same time.

"I did!" Tim exclaimed. "We played twenty-one for at least an hour."

"An hour? It took you an hour to play a game of twenty-one?" Jaxon laughed again.

"Naw, boy! You know your old man better than that. We played a bunch of games in an hour. I won pert' near all of 'em, too!"

Neither Jaxon nor Amanda believed Tim.

Moving past what his dad said about them playing basketball, Jaxon asked, "What did he say about me?"

Tim emphatically said, "Boy, I ain't lyin' to you. He didn't say a word about you."

Amanda interjected at this point. "You know he didn't come all the way over here and didn't even talk about Jax. You mean, you forgot what he said?"

Jaxon interjected again, "Dad, seriously! What did he say? Does he want me to play for the Angels or what?"

Tim threw his nose in the air as he turned his back toward everyone. "Fine! Y'all don't believe me. But he didn't say a word. We just played ball, he invited me to Pain, and then he left. Simple as that. Not only did he not mention you," he said as he pointed at Jaxon, "but I don't think he was too impressed with you either." He then pointed toward Amanda. "Y'all can just be jealous all you want." Tim smiled and left the room.

Amanda and Jaxon just looked at each other, got up, and followed Tim into the other room. "Would you be serious for a minute?" Amanda asked.

"I *am* being serious," Tim said. "He didn't say anything, not a word about it. I know that man didn't drive all the way over here because he heard I was the coolest cat around, but he sho' 'nuff didn't say anything about Jax." Tim imitated shooting a basketball. "I guess he was too impressed with my jumper to remember why he was really here."

Used to Tim constantly joking around, Amanda finally turned to Jaxon and said, "Son, don't worry about it. We'll find out eventually. Coach Davis is too busy of a man to drive all the way here just to shoot the breeze with your dad. He'll be back."

Still not sure who to believe, Jaxon said, "Well, if Coach Davis really was here, I can't wait to meet him. I hope I get to play for the Angels. I would love to be close enough for y'all to come see me play all the time."

Changing his tone to a more serious nature, Tim quickly said, "Son, I know you do. In fact, I'd be tickled pink if you played that close to home so me and your momma could watch all your home games. But you need to go into your senior year with an open mind about your options. The way you've been playing, there's gonna be a lot of teams after you. You'll need to carefully weigh all your options at all the schools that interest you. You're gonna need to do that based on what's best for you, not just because you love the Angels. You need to listen to what all of them have to say, and more importantly, what they aren't saying. You gotta pay attention, see what each culture is like, and make a decision that will determine your future. This ain't something you mess around with. You understand?"

Jaxon replied, "Yes, sir. I understand."

# 15
## A New Type of Leader

As Jaxon continues lying on the field, he can hear the concern in his coach's voice. "How we lookin'?" Coach Davis asks of the training staff. He knows it isn't good and won't look directly at Jaxon for any length of time, because he also has to keep his mind focused on the game. He is worried that if he makes eye contact with Jaxon, because of his father/son-like bond with him, he won't be able to keep from becoming emotional.

One of the trainers looks up at the coach and shakes his head with concern all over his face. Coach Davis now realizes this isn't a normal coach's visit to a fallen player. The look on the trainer's face says it all. His star player and honorary son isn't going to be getting up on his own.

Realizing how potentially serious the injury is, Coach Davis works his way through the crowd of training staff so he can see his player's face. He manages to get close to Jaxon while not preventing the athletic trainers from doing their best to care for him. As the coach positions himself where he can make eye contact with Jaxon, he says, "Son, I'm here. You hang in there! You hear me?"

Jaxon doesn't say a word, but he looks directly into Coach Davis's eyes and shows a very slight grin. Jaxon wants to say to his coach that he is fine, but the words won't come. He continues to look at Coach Davis and the look on his face isn't giving Jaxon a lot of reassurance. It is the first time Jaxon has ever seen that look on his coach's face. Coach Davis says to Jaxon, "You're gonna be fine, Bull. You hang in there. We're gonna get you up in a minute and get you some help."

Jaxon thinks, *That's the first lie Coach Davis has ever told me.* He can tell by the way everyone is acting that he isn't going to be fine, and he isn't going to be getting up on his own. He doesn't know how bad the injury is, but he knows it is bad. As he looks into his coach's eyes, he thinks back to the first time he met Coach Davis.

"So, you're the Bull," Coach Davis said to Jaxon as he reached out to shake Jaxon's enormous hand. "Man, I've heard a lot about you, and they weren't kidding."

It was Jaxon's first official recruiting trip to meet with the East Mississippi head coach, but it was far from his first recruiting trip. Jaxon's earlier recruiting trips had been eye opening and mostly uncomfortable for the naive boy from Tishomingo, Mississippi.

When he first started getting recruited, he was visiting schools from all over the country. He was visiting these schools at the same time as other potential athletes for each school. It wasn't until his senior year that he started getting the sole attention on his recruiting trips. Up until then, the recruiters thought they would partner him up with other five-star athletes, hoping to tempt them to play together.

Clearly, a lot of the earliest recruiters thought they would entice Jaxon by being the first to pursue his talents and recruiting very aggressively. Unfortunately for them, they didn't do their homework on the young man. Many of the first recruiting trips he took made Jaxon very uncomfortable and uninterested.

His first recruiting trip had been to a major program up north, and they partnered Jaxon with two other high school studs and one of the most beautiful girls Jaxon had ever seen. The young lady who was with the three boys was a college junior and the best recruiter they had. She was known for reeling in the best recruits for the football, basketball, and baseball teams with her undeniable charm and stunning beauty.

As she showed Jaxon and the other boys around, he mostly kept quiet and paid attention to everything around him. He was younger than the other recruits, and they were already used to receiving the royal treatment by the recruiters. They kept making jokes about the parties and the girls they were anticipating and didn't seem too interested in listening to where the chemistry building was located. They were interested in a completely different type of chemistry.

Later that evening, they all ended up going to one of the famous parties the other recruits were talking about. Jaxon was used to parties, but he felt like a complete foreigner in this particular one. There was an excitement level and energy at this party he had never felt back home. The music was loud, there were gorgeous girls everywhere he looked, and he was the youngest person there. Because of his stature, he didn't look like a high school student, and the girls certainly took notice of him. It was no secret that he was a valuable recruit, so the girls were all showing an interest in him, which made him uncomfortable and enthusiastic at the same time. He loved the attention but also felt conflicted.

Jaxon got his first taste of alcohol at the party that night. It was unintentional, but he tasted it, nonetheless. As he was being introduced to some of the current football players at the party, he noticed a beautiful girl approaching the group. Jaxon spotted her immediately and couldn't stop looking at her as she worked her way through the crowd of college athletes. Everyone seemed to know her, and she was clearly very popular on campus. When she made eye contact with

Jaxon, she said, "Well, hello there. Welcome to my house. I don't believe we've been introduced, and you don't have a drink in your hand."

Jaxon nervously smiled at the stunning host and said, "Thank you."

The young woman waited to see whether Jaxon was going to say anything else, and as he stood there with a goofy grin on his face, she said, "Well, you're welcome," and then she walked away.

That was all he could manage to say, and the other players all busted out laughing at him as she departed the group. He was so overwhelmed by her that he couldn't think of anything better to say. Once she was out of hearing distance, he jokingly started telling the other guys to shut up and was laughing with them about freezing up. He started talking big and saying that if he had the chance again, he would be smoother the next time.

After a few minutes of joking with one another about the experience, Jaxon was unaware of the young lady approaching him from behind. She spun him around and planted a big kiss on him, which caught him completely by surprise. Not only was the kiss an unexpected experience, but she also had a shot of alcohol in her mouth, which she passed along to him during their brief, intimate moment. Because Jaxon had no idea what was being forced into his mouth, he pushed away from her and violently spewed the drink all over the room. He backed away, wiping his mouth, and appeared disgusted by the encounter. Everyone started laughing even harder.

"Yeah! Much smoother this time!" said one of the football players as he was laughing uncontrollably while holding up the "okay" sign with his fingers. Jaxon was embarrassed, nervous, and ashamed as he quickly left the house. He could hear everyone laughing hysterically as the door closed behind him.

Jaxon wasn't too thrilled with his first recruiting trip, but he was eager to meet with the coach the next day and put the party behind him. As he was being escorted to the coach's office by the recruiter, he heard a girl's voice say, "I'll take him from here." As he looked up, he saw that it was the young lady from the party. Jaxon's face immediately became hot and red.

He started to talk, and all he could manage was, "I ... I ... I ..." before being interrupted by the young lady, who happened to be the student worker who worked for the head coach's office.

She said, "I've never had anyone react that way to one of my kisses. I must be losing my touch."

Jaxon quickly pulled himself together and said, "No, ma'am. I'm so sorry about that. That was my fault completely. I should never have allowed myself to be in that position."

She looked stunned. "Ma'am? Did you just call me 'ma'am'? No wonder you acted that way. You must think I'm an old woman."

Jaxon, nervous again, said, "No, ma'am. That's just what we say where I'm from."

She gave him a long look and said, "Well, I don't like it. That means you're old where I'm from. To make up for calling me old, rejecting my kiss, and spitting all over my house, I need you to do me a favor."

"Yes, ma'am. Uhh ... sorry. I mean ... okay. What do you want me to do?" Jaxon asked.

She said, "I work for Coach, and I was supposed to show you a good time last night. I didn't expect you to run out of my house when I kissed you, so I didn't get a chance to even really talk to you. Will you please tell Coach that you had a great time at my house party last night? I might get fired if you tell him what really happened."

Jaxon became uncomfortable again and began fidgeting as he stood before her. "I can't lie to him," Jaxon said as he stared at the ground. He continued speaking as if he were a little boy in trouble. "I won't lie for you or anyone else."

"Please!" she pleaded. "Coach told me yesterday that he was going to help me get a job when I graduate, so I can't afford to mess this up."

Up to this point on the trip, Jaxon had been so caught up in the emotion of being courted by this big-time program; he hadn't been relying on the values and lessons from his upbringing. He was acting completely like a fish out of water. He pulled himself together, reached for her hand, and said, "I have an idea. How about we do something together right now that will make up for last night and not make me a liar?"

She took a step back, her face got red, and her immediate response was, "Not in here!"

Jaxon started laughing and said, "Not *that*! Sorry. That's not what I meant. Give me your hand." As he reached for her hand, he could tell she wasn't sure what he had in mind. He sensed she had a history of being used by guys for her appearance, and his goal was to establish a connection of trust with her.

In a trip filled with awkwardness and embarrassment, Jaxon went back to what he knew best. "Allow me to pray over you. The coach can offer you a job, but I can offer you something far better. Do you know who Jesus is?"

The young lady appeared confused. She just gave Jaxon a blank stare for a few moments and said, "Yes. I mean … I know who He is. I mean … I've heard of Him."

Jaxon said, "Well, if you will allow me, I would love to ask Him to watch over you and help you fulfill what He has in store for you."

She just continued to stare at him, totally confused. She had never experienced anything like this with a boy, especially a highly sought-after recruit. She didn't say a word as he began to pray for her.

As he prayed for her, he thanked the Lord for allowing him to meet her, for who she was in Jesus, and asked Him to provide a future for her that would bring glory to His name. She had never heard anyone say the kinds of things he was saying about her. Jaxon said that Jesus loved her; she was a child of God. God desired a relationship with her, and she was special to Him. When he finished praying over her, he began explaining to her how much God loved her and what Jesus had done for her on the cross.

As he told her these things, he could see there were tears forming in her eyes and that she was on the verge of crying. It had been a long time since she had been to church, and all the emotions of her childhood were welling up inside her. She knew she had turned away from God while in college, and she was ashamed that she had lost touch with the God who created her. He could tell the message of what he was saying was sinking in with her, so he asked her whether she wanted to have a relationship with Jesus. She couldn't say a word, but she nodded in agreement to what he was asking.

He smiled and gently said, "This is the best decision you'll ever make. You don't have to say this exactly, but you can repeat after me if you would like. If you mean the words that we are about to say, Jesus will come into your life, and you will be a new person. Are you ready for that?"

She nodded again, and Jaxon said, "Great. Bow your head, and let's talk to Him."

He said these words, and she repeated everything he said. "Lord, I am so thankful for who You are and for what You have done for me. I know I am a sinner and that You died on the cross for my sins. I know You are the Son of God, and by me putting my faith in You, I will spend eternity with You in heaven. Lord Jesus, please forgive me of my sins and come into my heart and allow me to be a faithful follower of Your word. I want to give my life over to You and live in a way that will bring You honor and glory. Thank You, Jesus, for Your love, Your grace, and Your mercy. Amen!"

After they had both finished the prayer together, the coach opened the door to his office and saw the two of them holding each other's hands; then they hugged one another tightly. He could see that his young, beautiful assistant was crying and laughing at the same time as she seemed to be expressing overwhelming gratitude toward Jaxon. The coach was used to the young boys becoming infatuated with his intoxicating siren, but this seemed totally different. He said, "You lovebirds break it up out here. Mr. Bull, come on in."

As Jaxon walked past the coach into his office, the coach gave a thumbs-up to the young lady, who was forever changed by the experience. The coach said, "Well, Jaxon, I can see y'all must have had a pretty good time last night. I can still remember my first college recruiting trip and the girl I fell in love with." He leaned back in his chair, put his hands behind his head, and started chuckling as he said, "Well, I was in love with her until my second recruiting trip. You know what I'm sayin'?" He then began reminiscing to Jaxon about all his sleazy college recruiting trips from when he was in high school. Little did he know that he was losing Jaxon with each braggadocios story.

The majority of interactions on Jaxon's recruiting trips were very typical; girls, parties, drinking, and bragging. The recruits were all trying to hook up with the recruiters, the current players were all trying to get the recruits drunk, and the coaches were all selling dreams of championships and a road paved with gold to the NFL. There were boosters everywhere, offering cash and incentives to help their alma mater win championships. The entire process felt very immoral and unethical to Jaxon.

Jaxon really disliked the majority of the recruiting process, and if it hadn't been for the opportunity to lead someone to Jesus on his first trip, he would probably have lost hope in even going on more recruiting trips. There were several recruiting trips where he met coaches, recruiters, and other members of the universities who seemed like they were quality people with great intentions, but the overall process just seemed wrong to him.

The reason he hit it off so well with Coach Davis was that Coach Davis didn't appear to be anything like the other coaches he had met over the course of his recruiting journey. He knew his dad liked him, and he spoke highly of him after their encounter in their yard while playing basketball, but Jaxon wanted to know what else was there.

Coach Davis said during their introduction, "Man, I've heard a lot about you, and they weren't kidding."

Jaxon followed this up with his usual comment about people referring to his stature. "Yeah, I'm pretty good size, I reckon."

"You're definitely built like a grown man. That's for certain. But that ain't what I'm talking about. I've heard that you carry yourself like a man who knows the Lord, loves the Lord, and represents Jesus like He wants everyone else to know the Lord. People like that have a distinct confidence you can spot a mile away."

Jaxon was taken back by the comment because he wasn't used to a college coach speaking so freely about religion. Coach Davis followed up his comments with, "And son … I can tell that you live it. From the way you treated everyone in this complex, from the front door to the time you walked into my office, it's obvious you carry yourself like a seasoned veteran. What a blessing to see a young man come into my office with a reputation beyond speed, strength, height, having kids, having drug habits, or beating his girlfriend. Don't get me wrong, though. Those boys all deserve second chances, and we hope to make good men out of them, but it's great to have one coming in with a clean record."

Coach Davis invited Jaxon to have a seat in the nice leather chair in his office, and then he sat on the edge of his desk directly in front of Jaxon. "Mr. Bull, Son, I'm not going to waste your time. You are young and have a long ways to go before you officially sign somewhere, but that time comes faster than you'll be ready for it. You'll blink, and before you know it, you'll be in college. I'll jump right to why you're in my office instead of out with the pretty young recruiters. The reputation you have is what my guys need. Don't misunderstand me. I want a championship, just like everyone else, and I believe you can get us there, but my players need an educated path to a better eternity, and I believe you can help lead them there."

Coach Davis walked over to a board in his office with a list of players' names. "Most of these guys don't come from the same kind of upbringing you did, and they are hard to reach. A coach can only do so much with these guys, but a solid teammate is a brother for life. As teammates, you develop life together. You are involved with the most intimate details of each other's lives. You have the opportunity to develop a special bond with your teammates, and that bond is something no coach will ever be able to develop with these young men. I need someone like you to lead this team—not just to championships but to know our Lord. I love these guys, and I want what is best for their lives. Football is something they do but not who they should be. I spent enough time with your dad to know where you come from and what kind of man you are. Football is one thing, but the salvation of my guys is another."

Jaxon still hadn't said a word and was completely drawn into what the coach was saying. Coach Davis seemed like a man who believed every word of what he was saying and wasn't just trying to recruit him. "Son, I'm not asking you to make a commitment to me or to this university."

Coach Davis pointed toward the door of his office. "What I would like for you to do is spend some time with the men in that locker room. I want you to really pray for them, pray for me as a leader of this team, and ask the Lord to lead you in the direction He wants you to go. I want you to ask Him to reveal to you what group of young men to associate yourself with and be a strong witness to them during your college years, because they will be your brothers for life and in eternity. Jaxon, regardless of where you play ball, you're going to be in the spotlight, and you're going to have a lot of people pulling for you. I'm going to go ahead and tell you now. If you take a stand for God, you will be scrutinized. You will have people trying to expose you as a fraud. You will have it harder than the other guys. Whether you play for me or someone else, you will be challenged. Are you up to that kind of challenge?"

Without missing a beat, Jaxon said, "Yes, sir! I am looking forward to that kind of challenge."

Coach Davis held up his hand. "Please take your time before you commit to that. You are a man among boys, and football is going to be the easy part. The challenge I'm asking you to commit to is the one that will be the hardest of your career. It will not be easy, and I will not try to convince you it will be. Can you be the face of a program, the face of a university, the voice of your teammates, and still face your momma when you go home? I'm not asking you to come play football here. I'm asking you to be something bigger than football. I have some real studs committed to play ball here, so I don't need another five-star as much as I need a northern star. I need someone to lead these guys to Jesus."

# 16
## Battle Tested, Joy Filled

As Coach Davis stands on the field with his head down, looking at his clipboard, he slowly raises his head. The first person Coach Davis makes eye contact with is a young lady standing on the sidelines, who works with the EMU cheerleaders.

Joy Battle works as the temporary cheerleader coach while in graduate school at East Mississippi. She was a cheerleader when she was an undergraduate student, and because the previous cheerleader coach moved away, there was a request for Joy to take over until a full-time coach could be secured.

Joy's attention is now locked in on Jaxon's position on the field. Because her responsibilities during the game are to be in position to help keep the cheerleaders on track and focused on their assignments, she isn't immediately aware of what has happened. She, like everyone else, heard the collective *ouuuuuu* sound as the massive hit occurred on the field, but she hadn't seen what happened.

She immediately scans the bench to see whether there is any sense of panic with the coaches. Once she sees her friend, BJ, take a knee and start praying, she knows to tell the cheerleaders to all drop to a knee as well. She remains standing to try to see who is down on the ground.

She has a terrible feeling in her gut and is always nervous anytime a player was down. As the players on the field start dropping to a knee, she is able to see Jaxon lying on the ground. The sight of Jaxon lying lifelessly on the field immediately brings tears to Joy's eyes. She stands there, watching and paralyzed in fear.

Joy Battle was an extremely beautiful and intelligent young lady. Jaxon spotted her as soon as he and Phoenix walked through the door at one of the parties Phoenix loved to attend. Her beauty stopped Jaxon in his tracks. It was Jaxon and Phoenix's sophomore year, and these two giants were already the kings of campus. Everyone knew them and wanted a piece of them wherever they went. Phoenix loved the attention and soaked up every minute of devotion from his fellow students. Jaxon was always cordial but was good at diverting the attention away from himself. Everywhere they went, both young men received a lot of attention from the girls. They were very popular. Meeting girls was never a problem for either of them.

As soon as Phoenix walked inside, he wrapped his arms around the first two girls who approached him, and he worked his way through the crowd of fun-loving students. Jaxon, still standing there, staring at Joy, was approached by several other students, all vying for his time. Joy made eye contact with Jaxon, and he smiled at her. She turned away, not showing any kind of interest in his smile or who he was. Joy was a cheerleader and knew who he was, but she didn't like, or want anything to do with, football players.

Joy had come to East Mississippi as a freshman and had a reputation as a party girl. She loved to go out with her friends and close the bars down every weekend. She loved to dance her heart out and occasionally have a few drinks, but she wasn't a promiscuous girl.

During her freshman year, she didn't have a boyfriend, but there were a lot of guys constantly trying to date her. Because Joy had such a party-girl reputation, there were a lot of assumptions and accusations about her private life. There were a lot of people who labeled her as a girl who hooked up a lot and slept around. In reality, she was a virgin who was saving herself for marriage. All her fellow cheerleaders and close friends knew this about her, but assumptions on campus seemed to be stronger than facts. The court of public opinion found her guilty.

It was late during her first year as a cheerleader when everything about her fun-loving, gentle spirit changed. The cheerleaders and all the male and female athletes on campus had mutual social circles and interacted regularly. They were all at the same parties and ran into each other all the time at dining halls, banquets, classes, and so forth. During Joy's entire first semester, she remained single and had no desire to date anyone. She was having fun enjoying her single life and college experience with her friends.

After the end of the football season, one of the seniors on the team, Trey, had an old high school friend in town from a smaller school's football team. Just like most other weekends, there were a bunch of athletes at a party just off campus. Joy was there, as she usually was, doing nothing to draw any negative attention to herself. She was just dancing and having a good time when Trey's friend, Alec, spotted her in the crowd. Because Alec didn't go to school there, he didn't know her, so he asked his friend about her.

Even though Joy was just a freshman and Trey was a senior, he still knew who she was. She was one of the most beautiful girls on campus, and everyone liked her. She was very popular by now, and her beauty, along with the mystery about her sex life, made her a topic of discussion among many of the male athletes.

Trey told his friend there were conflicting stories about her. He told Alec she was a freshman, she liked to party, and some people said she hooked up a lot, but nobody knew with whom. He said he had also heard that she wouldn't sleep with anyone, but he wasn't sure which was true. Trey jokingly confirmed, "The only thing I know for certain is that I haven't slept with her … yet!"

Alec was laser focused on Joy at this point. As Trey continued to speak, Alec had tuned him out, and he thought only about how to approach Joy. While Trey was still talking, Alec made his move as soon as he saw Joy step away from her friends. He acted like a lion approaching his prey, which had just been separated from the heard. Alec was used to girls giving him lots of attention, because he was a popular athlete at his school, so he advanced toward Joy with plenty of confidence.

As she was cooling down from dancing, Alec walked up to her and introduced himself. "Hi. I'm Alec. What's your name?"

Joy energetically responded, "Hey, Alec, I'm Joy. Nice to meet you. Sorry, I'm so sweaty from dancing." She quickly wiped her hand on the napkin from her drink, then reached out to shake his hand and asked, "How come I've never seen you before? You don't look familiar."

Sensing the sincere sweetness in Joy, Alec responded with, "I don't go to school here. I'm here visiting one of my buddies, but when we got here, he left me. I don't know anybody here. I was thinking about leaving, because I'm shy and parties make me uncomfortable."

Feeling sorry for Alec, Joy said, "Don't leave. Why would you leave so much fun?"

"It's not fun if you don't know anyone, and nobody wants to talk to you."

Joy smiled really big and said, "You know me now. You're talking to me. Don't leave. I can't believe your friend left you. That's so mean."

Taking advantage of Joy's kindness, Alec asked her to go outside with him so he could hear her better while they talked. Joy, thoroughly scanning the crowd to verify where her friends were, spotted them and made eye contact with several of them. She did this to try to safeguard herself; they knew who she was with before she went outside.

He took her by the hand and led her outside. There were a lot of people at the party, including her friends, who saw her holding hands with this stranger and leaving the party together. Once they got outside, Alec told Joy how sweet she was for being willing to step away from something she was certainly enjoying to help a stranger feel more comfortable. He was being very charming and sweet to Joy. Alec was an attractive guy, and because he was being so nice, Joy enjoyed being with him.

After talking a while, he said, "You are so sweet to come out here with me. I'm sorry you're missing your party to babysit some loser who got left by his friend."

"You're not a loser!" Joy exclaimed. "You're very nice. I don't know why anyone would leave you. You're too sweet." She was doing her best to comfort Alec, who appeared sad at his make-believe misfortune.

Alec continued, "I guess I'm going to try to walk back to my friend's apartment, if I can even find it. I just hope he's there and lets me inside."

"Why?" Joy asked. "You don't want to stay here?"

"I don't want to keep you away from the party. I don't want to be a bother, so I'm going to go. If I'm not here, you won't have to be bored outside with me." Joy was falling right into Alec's trap.

"You don't have a car? Why would you have to walk?" Joy inquired.

"No. I rode with my friend, and I don't know when he will be back.

I'm just ready to go. You've been so nice to me. I really hope I get to see you again, if I ever come back."

Joy wasn't happy that Alec seemed so sad. "Why would you not come back?"

"I just didn't have a good time tonight. I didn't meet anyone that was nice until I met you. I'm just ready to go back home."

Joy said, "I'll take you to his apartment. I'll give you a ride. I'm gonna give him a piece of my mind. He shouldn't have left you. You can't leave campus thinking we are all bad. I'll make sure you know there are nice people here."

Alec smiled and grabbed Joy's hand. He then leaned in and kissed her on the cheek. "You are the sweetest person I've ever met."

As the two got in Joy's car and drove away, he kept apologizing to her for being a nuisance and doing his best to make her feel sorry for him even more. When they got to the apartment, Alec, knowing his friend was still at the party, said, "Well, if you still wanna give him a piece of your mind, I'll walk you up there. I understand if you don't feel comfortable though."

Joy sat and thought for a moment, and Alec could sense she was calming down by now and was smart enough not to go inside the apartment with a perfect stranger. "I wouldn't blame you for not wanting to go up there with me. I am a pretty big and scary-looking guy."

Not wanting to seem like she was judging him or afraid of him, Joy said, "You know what? I am going to give him a piece of my mind. Let's go. Lead the way."

When they got inside the apartment, Alec pretended to search for his friend but was obviously and predictably unsuccessful. As Alec sat down on the couch, he said, "He must have gone home with some girl. I don't know why he does stuff like that. He should really show more respect for women than what he does. He will probably be here soon.

He just does what he wants with them and comes right home. I try to be a good example, but I can see it's gonna take more work."

Impressed with how sensitive Alec was with the concern he showed for his friend, Joy decided to wait. "Well, if he won't be long … I'll wait here with you. He needs to hear what I have to say. He shouldn't treat people like this."

She walked over to the couch and sat down near Alec. After they talked for a while, Alec continued pouring on the lies, and he eventually made his move. They started kissing and were both enjoying themselves for the moment.

Alec then asked if Joy would like to join him in the bedroom, and she said, "I think we better stay out here."

Alec tried to reassure her. "I just don't want anyone to walk in on us kissing." He tried to imply that was all he had in mind. After she refused, he began trying to kiss her again.

Joy said, "I should probably get going. I'm sure my friends are worried about me." Alec asked her to stay a little while longer as he pulled her closer to him. She said as she pushed his hands away and stood to her feet, "I really need to get going. I'm sorry. I shouldn't have come up here."

Alec could sense he wasn't going to convince her to stay or go into the bedroom with him, so he didn't allow her to leave. Alec violently forced her back down on the couch and stole Joy's innocence. He robbed from her the gift she had intended to save only for her future husband. She was terrified and heartbroken.

They both heard the front door open, and Alec immediately let go of Joy. Joy was so afraid and embarrassed that she shot out of the apartment like a bolt of lightning. Trey got the sense that something was wrong with her, but he just assumed Joy didn't want him to recognize her. As she ran out of the apartment, she slammed the door behind her.

Trey was still standing at the door with a confused expression when he turned, pulled the curtain back, and looked out the window.

He quickly spun his head back to see Alec, pointed out the window, and asked, "Was that?" He didn't finish his own sentence when he stopped to say, "Nah!" He paused again and said with a sound of disbelief, "Wait! Was that Joy? The cheerleader? How in the world did you get her over here?"

Alec, still sitting on the couch, said, "I didn't. She got me over here. She brought me here, and we just got finished getting to know one another better when you came in and messed things up."

Trey was impressed and in disbelief that his friend had been able to get one of the best-looking girls in school back to his apartment on his first night in town. "You ol' dog, you! You must have really sharpened your skills since high school. How did you do that? Did y'all really … Y'all didn't?" Trey shook his head in bewilderment.

It was that night when the sweet innocence about Joy was taken away and replaced with anger and resentment. She began to hate football players, because of that terrible action taken by a stranger in town and the disgusting stories that followed. Alec left the next day and never returned to Pain, but the damage he'd inflicted remained for years.

Because Trey walked in on what he assumed to be a mutual encounter and because everyone at the party saw Joy leaving while Alec was holding her hand, everyone believed Joy was secretly sexually active. During her entire college experience up to this point, Joy felt like she'd had nothing to prove and consistently maintained her reputation as someone unwilling to have premarital sex. But after word spread about her encounter with Alec, there were a lot of people who believed she was a liar and was just pretending to be a "good girl." False rumors quickly spread that she slept only with people from out of town to maintain a fake reputation on campus.

Joy was hurt and angry. She didn't want anyone to know she had been raped. In her mind, she believed it was her fault. Her anger overwhelmed her because she had known better than to go with him and had even gone against her instincts by going inside the apartment with him. Joy didn't believe anyone would believe her if she tried explaining what had happened, so she never told law enforcement or college officials. The once-spirited and sweet cheerleader never even mentioned that night to any of her teammates, friends, or family.

Joy became a very different person after that night. She was angry—not only with herself but with God. She believed that He had allowed the rape to happen to her and it made her furious. She refused to go back to church and became upset anytime someone even asked her to go, but she never explained why.

At parties Joy became the exact opposite of what she had always been before. She became a heavy drinker and was often out of control. She became joyless and eventually started living up to her originally undeserved reputation. Her new party routine consisted of often leaving parties with strangers from out of town, who were there visiting friends. Over time she became increasingly physical with guys, trying to numb any sense of who she was. She never spent time with the same guy twice, because she engaged only with strangers. She felt embarrassed, ashamed, broken, and alone.

When Jaxon spotted her at the party that night, she was two years older than he, so she was a senior at this point in her college career. He knew nothing about her reputation or who she was. He just knew she was beautiful, and he was instantly drawn to her.

As other students greeted Jaxon at the party, he saw one of his female friends, Amy, he knew from FCA. He immediately inquired about the beautiful girl. After he hugged Amy, he kept his arm over her shoulder and asked, "Do you know who that girl is?" as he motioned toward Joy.

Amy responded, "Bull, you're so sweet. You're always trying to save someone, aren't you?"

"What do you mean?"

"You are talking about that girl over there, aren't you?" Amy pointed in Joy's direction.

"Yeah. Why does she need saving?"

Amy surprisingly asked, "You don't know who that is? She's a cheerleader. I thought all you jugheads knew who the cheerleaders were, especially ones that look like her."

"No ma'am," Jaxon responded. "I've never met her, and I don't know anything about her. What's her name?"

Amy smiled at him briefly, then said with a warning look, "She's a senior. Rumor is, she used to be one of the sweetest and most godly girls on campus but not anymore. Her name is Joy, and from what I've heard, she isn't the kind of gal you want to take home to your momma. Supposedly she has had more one-night stands than anyone on campus. I personally don't know anyone who has actually gone out with her or dated her, but that is the word on the street. I just figured you were going to try to save her. I've gotta warn ya. I know it's kind of your thing, but I hear she gets really mad if you ask her to go to church."

"That's interesting," Jaxon said as he continued to look at Joy with an expression of interest.

Ignoring Amy's advice, Jaxon made his way over to Joy. As he approached her, he could see she was drinking straight whiskey. He walked up behind her, tapped her on the shoulder, and said, "Hi, I'm Jaxon."

Joy turned her head so she could see Jaxon and said, "Good for you!" Then she turned back away from him. He was dumbfounded and intrigued by her coldness toward him, because people were typically receptive to his greetings.

He took a couple of steps to his right to position himself better in her line of sight and asked, "What's your name?"

Joy gave another short and pointed answer. "Not interested."

Jaxon was not one to take defeat easily. "That's a very pretty and unique name you've got there. I've known a lot of double-named girls in my life, but I've never heard that one before."

Joy found the comment funny but didn't want to appear amused or seemingly interested. "Look, I don't sleep with football players, so stop bothering me."

Being quick witted since he was a kid, he said, "What a coincidence! Me neither. We have a lot in common." At his comment, Joy gave a slight chuckle and looked up at him with an expression of aggravation.

"What do you want? I told you, I don't mess with football players," Joy sternly said.

Jaxon flashed his big smile. "Would you like me to quit? I can play other sports. I bet I would make a good cheerleader. If I became a cheerleader, you'd have to talk to me then."

Joy started to laugh again and said, "No, I don't wanna be responsible for that. You'd be the first Heisman cheerleader."

"So, you *do* know who I am?"

"Yeah, I know who you are. But I still don't know what you want. Trust me, I'm not your type,"

"What's my type?" Jaxon asked.

Joy responded while throwing up some air quotes. "The 'religious type.' You like good girls, and you only invite girls like me to church to try to make them your type. I'll tell you right now, *church boy*, that's not me, and that ain't happening."

Jaxon realized that getting to know her was going to be a bumpy and long journey. He smiled again and said, "Well, that's not true at all. I also invite guys to church. Besides, I don't even like the religious type."

He knew that answer would throw her for a loop and potentially cause her to ask the question. He could tell by her expression that she was confused by him saying he didn't like the "religious type." Nobody could watch a press conference, a sports news station, or hear anything about Jaxon without also hearing the name of Jesus. She assumed there wasn't a more "religious type" person on campus than him.

The longer Jaxon interacted with her, the more interested in him she became. She was still very hardened, so she decided it would be in her best interest to get away from Jaxon. She did what very few had ever done before; she stared directly at his big smile and walked away. She walked right past him without saying another word. Jaxon turned and said, "It was great meeting you, 'Not Interested!' I can't wait to see you again!"

Over the next couple of months, Jaxon did everything he could to cross paths with Joy on campus. Almost daily he encountered her at the dining hall and offered to pay for her lunch. He did this, knowing her lunch was already paid for once she was inside the dining facility. She found it funny each time, but every time she said, "It's already paid for, you idiot. Now leave me alone."

Jaxon followed up the lunch rejection with, "How about dinner? Maybe meet up for some ice cream?" Over time her rejections sounded less mean and nasty, and became more playful.

Each day people looked at them and wondered what was going on between them. Everyone was confused why it seemed like Jaxon, who hadn't dated anyone up to this point, would continuously flirt with Joy. Joy had a terrible reputation and didn't seem like the kind of girl Jaxon would pursue. Jaxon hadn't gone on one date or even appeared to be interested in anything but football and working out since he arrived on campus.

Also, nobody could figure out why Joy would turn down his advances. Every girl on campus would trade places with her in a heartbeat. Why would she pass up an opportunity to be with someone who could instantly repair her reputation? Their actions confused the entire campus. Not only was the whole campus curious when she showed up on the cover of a famous sports magazine, standing next to Jaxon; the rest of the nation became inquisitive.

Jaxon was running on campus one beautiful spring Saturday morning when he spotted Joy reading in "the Orchard." The Orchard is a beautiful wooded area in the heart of campus. Students congregate there to study, throw football, or just hang out with their friends. It was less than a week away from Joy's graduation and the end of Jaxon's sophomore year.

As he was running, he spotted her from a distance and started walking her direction. She was beautiful. She was sitting on the freshly cut green grass, leaning against one of the massive old trees. She had her hair pulled back in a ponytail and wore a tank top and some running shorts. There was a perfect ray of sunshine beaming down on her like a spotlight, directing Jaxon right toward her.

"What cha reading?" Jaxon asked as he approached her. Joy recognized Jaxon's voice and immediately smiled but didn't raise her eyes. "You studying or reading for fun? It's way too beautiful to be reading on a morning like this."

Jaxon continued without seeming discouraged. He had spent the entire semester making multiple attempts at conversation with Joy before she finally responded. By this time of the year, they were both used to the routine, but both enjoyed the dance.

Joy slowly lifted her eyes from the book to make eye contact.

"How'd you find me? Isn't it too beautiful of a morning to be out running and getting all nasty?" she said in response to Jaxon's question.

"Girl, I've been running all over this town, huntin' for you. You are easy to find, just hard to catch up with. I just follow the sound of cranky."

"I'm not cranky!"

"You can be with me," Jaxon shot back. "I can't tell if you're more 'Joy' or 'Battle' when I'm around."

Joy couldn't help but laugh. "I guess I've given you a pretty hard time this semester," she said as she lowered her head back to her book.

"Nah. You're just playing hard to get. You gotta keep in mind, though, I'm not a quitter."

Joy looked back at Jaxon and asked, "Why me? Why have you spent so much time trying to talk to me this semester? I've done nothing to make you think I'm interested. I've never been nice to you. Why do you keep being so nice to me?"

Jaxon continued to stare down at Joy, reached his hand out, and said, "Come with me."

She grabbed his hand and he pulled her up. "Where are we going?"

Jaxon replied, "I'm going to show you the answer to your question."

Jaxon turned her around, put his hand on her shoulder, and pointed to a tree, where two branches intersected with the trunk.

"A tree?" Joy responded. "You're being nice to me because of a tree?"

He just smiled and said, "Be patient." He gently took her hand and held it as he walked her over to the stage in the Orchard and pointed to a cross section of the structure. He asked her, "What do you see there?"

Joy, sounding confused at this point, said, "A beam?"

Jaxon smiled. "Be patient with me." While still holding her hand, he continued leading her across the Orchard until they saw a young married couple holding hands and swinging their daughter between them. "How about that? What do you see there?" He pointed at the young family.

"I see a little girl having fun with her parents. What are you talking about?"

Jaxon smiled and said, "Just a little longer. Keep being patient with me." He walked her over to an open spot and pointed to the beautiful, blue sky and asked, "What about there? What do you see?"

Joy quickly responded with, "The sky. What on earth are you talking about? What does any of that have to do with me?"

"You see a bunch of random things in the beauty in front of you, but I see Jesus. I see Jesus in everything."

Joy started to pull her hand away from Jaxon, but he gently pulled her back toward him as he continued. "I see Him, because I am looking for Him. From the first moment I saw you, I saw Jesus in you. I have not been able to take my eyes off you since I first spotted you. You are beautiful. Everyone sees your external beauty, but I see more. There is something about you that God has drawn me to, and I've never experienced anything like it before."

Not liking the direction of the conversation, Joy stood there with a frustrated expression on her face. "Jaxon, you've been the nicest guy to me, and I am so thankful for how you've treated me, but I told you when we met. I'm not the religious type. Don't try to make me be that type."

Jaxon smiled and said, "I know. You remember my response to that? You ready to ask me the question now?"

"What question?"

"The question you wanted to ask me then and still want to ask me now."

Joy paused and thought for a moment. "Why do you not like the religious type?"

"That's the right question," Jaxon responded. "The same reason

Jesus didn't. I like the 'relational type,' the type who won't judge someone because of their past but will look at their heart and treat others how Jesus would treat them. I try my best to be the kind of person who treats everyone the same. I don't want to ever be confused with the 'religious type,' the type of people known for looking down on others and holding people to rules they can't even follow themselves. We are all just people, and I'm not being critical of people like that, because we all need to do better. But I want to be the type who lifts others up and loves them the way they are. I leave changing hearts up to Jesus. I just try to love people as best I can."

Having been raised in the church, Joy knew what Jaxon was talking about but still wasn't softening. "If you really knew me, you'd think differently about me. You wouldn't be seen talking to me. You'd keep running. I'm not like you, Jaxon. I'm not perfect."

"You know what?" Jaxon said. "Jesus knows us both, and He loves us both. He loves us exactly the same. He doesn't love me any more or less than He loves you. I know you're not perfect. I hope you realize I'm not perfect either. To Him, you *are* perfect. We both have things in our lives He wants us to change, but He still loves us. Jesus loves you, Joy."

With tears in her eyes, Joy lowered her head, and said "It's my fault, Jaxon."

In spite of being sweaty from his run, he still pulled her close to him and held her tight. He didn't say a word. He knew she was hurting and needed some time to process what they had just talked about. He just held her and let her cry. Nobody had taken the time to really express that kind of love to her in a long time. After she was raped by Alec, she'd felt dirty and alone. With her heart hardened and her reputation falsely ruined, she became the image her peers unfairly put on her.

She felt that all her "religious type" friends had turned their backs on her and treated her like she no longer belonged. She developed a whole new identity. Her friends were different, she rarely visited her family, and she became what a lot of people wanted her to become. She was very popular, but on the inside, she was miserable.

Jaxon had spent the entire semester talking to her nearly every day, and not once had he come across as judgmental or anything more than a gentleman; he'd won over her confidence. It was the first time she had ever mentioned what happened to her. Upon voicing the words "It's my fault," she released tension and fears she had been carrying since she was a freshman.

Jaxon didn't ask what she meant, but he knew it was something that haunted Joy. After crying for a moment and staring at the ground, she felt a sense of relief, but still did not want to talk. To help release the built-up tension, she looked at Jaxon and asked, "Do you mind if I run with you?"

Jaxon smiled. "Just don't try to outrun me. Like I said, I'm not a quitter." Jokingly, he continued "Nobody knows this, but I have a bit of a competitive streak in me."

They ran for hours that morning. They talked, laughed, and ran until they had covered nearly the entire town of Pain. They became inseparable that day. Joy graduated the next weekend but stayed in town for the summer, because she was still uncertain about her plans for the future.

That summer the EMU cheerleader coach resigned, and the athletic department was in need of a new cheerleader coach. Because Joy was around all summer, she and Jaxon were regularly seen all over campus and town. One of the senior athletic administrators, Kim, stopped Jaxon and Joy one day on campus as they were finishing up their normal afternoon run and asked Joy what her future plans were. Joy told Kim she had taken the graduate school test but was still unsure whether she was going to go to graduate school or just get a job. Fortunately, Joy was extremely intelligent, and she had already been accepted to several graduate programs. Because she was still undecided, she hadn't accepted any of the school or job offers she had received.

"Did you apply for graduate school here?" Kim asked.

"Yes, ma'am. I got accepted, but I haven't officially enrolled. I don't want to take on any debt, and I'm not asking anyone to help me with school."

"How about we pay for it?" Kim asked.

"What do you mean? Why would you do that?"

Kim said, "Well, I think we can help each other out. You need your school to be paid for, and I need a cheerleader coach. If we pay for you to get your graduate degree, you can be our new coach while you're in school. How's that sound?" Kim glanced over at Jaxon, as if not even aware of his presence until then, and said, "Oh, hey, Bull."

Jaxon smiled at Joy and said, "That sounds pretty good to me!"

Joy glanced back at him. "I don't know." She turned back to Kim and said, "Thank you so much for thinking of me and asking me, but do you mind if I think about it?"

Kim agreed but told Joy she needed an answer fairly soon, because she needed to find someone else if Joy wasn't interested.

As Joy and Jaxon walked away, she kept her head down, and he could tell she was in deep thought. "What's up? You wanna talk about it?" Jaxon asked.

Joy kept walking quietly until they reached the parking lot. She leaned against a car and said, "I don't think this is a good idea."

Jaxon asked why she thought that, and she said, "They all know me. They know what I've done and who I am. I feel like I need to start over somewhere new. I don't want to be that person anymore. They won't have any respect for me, and I'll be a joke to them."

Jaxon smiled and pulled her in close. "I know who you are. I know what you've done. I'm ready for you to start something new too. I want you to start something new, with me. Joy, you are who I want—not just who you can be but who you really are. I don't want you to leave. If you stay here for graduate school, we can be together. And don't worry about the other cheerleaders. You have such an amazing impact on your team. They would do anything for you."

Joy faced Jaxon and said, with tears in her eyes, "You don't know me. If you did, you'd run away screaming."

Jaxon said, "Joy, I pray a lot. I pray for you a lot. I have been praying for you since we met. In some ways, I've been praying for you since *before* we met. I prayed this morning and asked the Lord to do something amazing if He wanted us to be together. I knew you were done with school and would possibly be leaving, but I prayed for Him to make a way for you to stay, if it was His will for us to be together. I don't believe Ms. Kim's asking you to stay is a coincidence. I believe God has something amazing in store for you here, and I am anxiously awaiting seeing His hand and mine holding yours as you experience it."

Joy was emotionally moved by Jaxon putting himself out there like that. She didn't feel worthy of the attention and admiration he showed her, but he never relented in his growing affection for her. She didn't say a word to him and walked into the athletic office to find Kim. She walked to her office and said, "I've thought about it long enough. I accept."

Over the next two years, Joy and Jaxon became the most popular couple on campus. They were quite possibly the most popular couple in the country. With his athletic stardom, constant media coverage, and amazing charm, he was the most beloved athlete in the country. It was no surprise that Joy was the most envied girl on campus, because of her relationship with Jaxon. Joy was no longer an undergraduate student, but she was still the most beautiful girl on campus. They were a fantastic couple.

They were a great match and loved each other very well, but Joy still didn't allow herself to become the "good girl" everyone thought she should be, just because she was dating Jaxon. She still wasn't interested in going to church, FCA, or the Bible studies Jaxon attended. Jaxon never pressured her but asked her and Phoenix to join him every weekend.

During Jaxon's junior season, he was unstoppable on the field. He was already a two-time Heisman winner and was on his way to winning a third. He was an instant lock for the first pick in the draft, and everyone was already talking about what his impact would be in the pros. All the talk about his impact really got Joy thinking about her impact. One evening while they were eating at a picnic table on campus, she said to him, "I don't have an impact."

Jaxon curiously peered down at his food and smiled at her with confusion. "I don't believe I have any either, but if you see some on my plate, you're welcome to it."

She said, "All I've been hearing about for the last couple of weeks is the impact you have and are going to have. I don't have an impact. I want to be impactful."

Jaxon said, "You impact me. You're very impactful to me."

Frustrated, Joy said, "I don't want to just be known as 'the Bull's girlfriend.' I want to be able to impact others. I want to do something that will leave an impact on others, like you do. You're so good with others. People feel completely different after spending time with you. You make people feel special. You really connect with people."

"You do," Jaxon said. "You impact people every day. Those cheerleaders really admire and respect you."

"Only because I'm your girlfriend."

"That's not true. They don't even care when I'm around. Why don't you go to FCA with me tonight? You'll see. To them, I'm just a normal guy. You are the one they look up to."

Joy asked, "They go to FCA? I never knew that."

Jaxon started laughing and said, "Well, you're not really known as a 'church-friendly' gal. People are scared to talk to you about church. You told me that when we first started hanging out, and I've witnessed it myself."

Joy, slightly embarrassed, laughed and said, "I'm not *that* bad! I'll go with you this time just to prove you wrong."

When she and Jaxon walked through the doors of the room where the Fellowship of Christian Athlete's met, she immediately recognized nearly everyone in the room. She was completely surprised by all those she saw in there. She saw people she knew partied a lot and people she'd thought would never go to such a thing.

As soon as the cheerleaders spotted her, they came running over to her. They were extremely excited to see her and couldn't believe she was there. Jaxon and Joy had arrived a little late, so everyone was already being broken into groups. The cheerleaders grabbed Joy and said, "Come be in our group," without even acknowledging that Jaxon was standing there. He just stared at her and gave her a look that said, *I told you.*

There were several small groups of four to five people per group in the room. Joy's group was composed of her and four female cheerleaders. The FCA leader was walking around the room with a hat in his hand, and when he got to the cheerleaders, the senior cheerleader, Becky, reached into the hat and pulled out a small piece of paper. She read the paper aloud. "Who has impacted you the most?"

The question paralyzed Joy. She couldn't believe what she had just heard. She and Jaxon had just finished that conversation, and here it was again. She sat there in total silence. Becky said, "Since I read the question and I feel God is showing me something unbelievable right now, I will be glad to go first."

She paused for a moment and started to cry. "Wow. I can't believe this." She sat there quietly for a moment, shaking her head. "God is so awesome!" She faced Joy and said, "Joy … it's you! I can't believe you are here right now. I've been coming to FCA since I was a freshman, and you've never been. I get this question, and now you're here. God is so awesome!"

Still sitting in silence and not believing what was happening, Joy started to tear up as well. She gently whispered, "Me?"

Becky responded, "Yes, Joy, you! I have admired you since I met you. I was scared to death when I got to campus. I was sexually assaulted the summer before I came to EMU, and I almost didn't come. When I got here and met you, I had never met such a strong girl in my life. You were a sophomore and were the toughest girl I had ever met. When we were on our way home from a game one night, I was sitting with you on the bus when I told you what had happened to me. You were the first person I ever told, and you made me feel safe. You made me feel like you truly understood and could relate somehow. I never knew how, but somehow you could actually feel my pain. That's what gave me the courage to start coming to FCA and eventually led me to Christ."

As soon as she finished talking, another cheerleader, a junior, said, "You're mine too, Joy. After my sister was beaten up in our apartment by her boyfriend and sent to the hospital, you were the only one who could help us get through that. She was living with me during her senior year, and she just wanted to leave school and get away from here. With him being on the football team at the time, you were the one who was brave enough to go to the coach and get him thrown off the team and expelled from school. You were the one who was able to help us get through it. My heart was so full, because of the way you fought for us. You spent so much time with us and encouraged us in so many ways. You can't believe how much my sister still talks about you. You are her hero! You helped her face her fears, and she stayed in school and graduated. She loves you! *I* love you!"

The last two cheerleaders were freshmen, and they had known Joy only as a coach. They also both said Joy was the one who had made the biggest impact on them. They had both considered going to cheer at other schools until they met Joy. They both felt so incredibly comfortable and safe around Joy. She had a confidence about her that they had never seen in a female. Her presence told them, without her having to say it, that she would always have their backs, no matter what. Unbeknownst to the group, all the girls had been sexually assaulted at some point in time or were very close to someone who had.

Joy had never shared with anyone what happened to her, but in that moment, she felt a peace she hadn't felt in many years. She knew God had called her there that night to hear their stories. She knew that her experience, as terrible as it was, allowed her to relate to and lead these girls. She knew she was able to understand their pain because she knew pain. It was the first time since that night when she no longer felt like she was to blame. She no longer felt like a victim. She felt stronger than ever and was grateful for these girls in her life.

To ease the seriousness of the moment, one of the girls made a joke by saying, "I guess what we are trying to say is, we are all in love with you, Joy!" They were all laughing, crying, and wiping their eyes when Joy glanced over at Jaxon. As soon as they made eye contact, she mouthed the words "Thank you" to Jaxon. He just smiled.

# 17
## The Interview

"Let's go down to the field and check with Ashley," the raspy old voice says from inside the booth high above the action. "Ashley, can you get a sense of what's going on? What can you tell us?"

Ashley, the award-winning sideline reporter, has been covering college football games for the entire length of Jaxon's college football career and is laser focused on Jaxon's position on the field. She has become known for asking great questions to coaches and players. She is and has always been great at getting these gridiron greats to open up and share things other reporters are unable to accomplish. Unlike many famous reporters, she is very professional and always keeps the focus of her interviews, on those she is interviewing. She is loved and respected by millions for not bringing any attention to herself but always making the other person feel like the most important person in the world.

"Can you hear us, Ashley?" the voice from above tries again. "Ashley, are you there? Sorry, folks, we must be having some technical difficulties."

Ashley isn't paying attention to anything except Jaxon. She knew as soon as the hit occurred that something is wrong. She is fortunate enough to cover many of the games Jaxon has played in during his career and has developed a meaningful friendship with him. As she stands here, staring in disbelief of his injury, she reflects on her nationally covered, sit-down interview with Jaxon. She can't help but think about the passion that was in his voice as he'd shared with her what was most important to him.

"Good evening!" Ashely said, staring directly into the camera. "We've titled this segment 'Know Bull!' I am here with a man who needs no introduction. He is by far the best athlete I have ever covered. He has won nearly every award college football has to offer. He is a lock as the number one pick in the NFL draft. In my opinion, he is the best college football player of all time. And from all accounts, he is an even better person off the field than he is a player on the field. More importantly to me, over the last few years, he has become a very dear friend of mine."

"Thank you, Ashley!" Jaxon laughed. "That is quite the introduction."

"Well, it's true," Ashley said before she took a deep breath, trying to calm her nerves. "So, Jaxon, it's great to be here with you this evening."

"Yes, ma'am. I agree. It's great to be here with you too, my friend."

"You always make me feel so old when you call me 'ma'am,'" Ashley responded. "You know, I'm not *that* much older than you."

Jaxon laughed. "I know. You've told me that before. Sorry about that. I hope you'll forgive me, because I'm going to have to keep using it. It's in my blood. Besides, I can't let my momma see this interview and not hear me saying, 'ma'am.'"

"I guess I'll let you slide," Ashley said as she nervously brushed hair away from her face. "Now, let's get started. First question. Why would you say that you are the greatest?"

Jaxon took a deep breath and smiled really big. "Well, Ashley, I wouldn't say that."

"You wouldn't?" Ashley seemed surprised. "There seems to be no doubt that you are. You hold records in nearly every category in which you are eligible."

Jaxon shifted from one side of his seat to the other, seemingly uncomfortable with the realization of the direction of the conversation. "Yes, ma'am. That is correct. But I wouldn't say that *I* am the greatest." He seemed as if he were baiting her in to asking the question.

Ashley, unsure of what Jaxon's answer would be, asked anyway. "If you are not the greatest, who would you say is the greatest?"

Jaxon sat a little taller in his chair and seemed ready to dive deeper into his answer. "Well, ma'am, Jesus is the greatest."

"Oh, I see." Ashley leaned back, raised her head, and slightly rolled her eyes, trying not to show her frustrations to the television camera. She quickly tried moving along to the next question, because she had been instructed to stay away from religious topics with Jaxon. Jaxon had always been known for praising God each time a microphone was in his face. The world was well aware of his beliefs and for whom he stood. Neither Ashley nor her bosses wanted this interview to turn in to a televised church sermon. Ashley and Jaxon had had several conversations over the years, and Ashley had been very adamant with Jaxon off the air that she didn't believe in God, heaven, Jesus, or anything religious.

She had always maintained her professionalism on air and not allowed Jaxon's comments about Jesus to slow her down from asking about football. She had always made it clear to him that she would rather him stick to the topics she asked him about, especially during this interview. This was her first chance to get off the sidelines to do a one-on-one interview, and she was eager to impress everyone with her interviewing skills.

Ashley tried to continue. "What I mean is—"

Jaxon interrupted Ashley before she could continue. He leaned forward and seemed to get excited about the topic he was about to discuss. "There never has and never well be anyone or anything greater. He is the author of all things. He is the forgiver of sins, and He makes all things new. He is the reason I am what I am. He is the reason you and I are face-to-face at this very moment. I experience grace and love through Him, which is unmatched by anyone or anything on earth."

Ashley made another attempt to move the conversation along, but there was a slight bit of frustration in her voice. "That's good. Good for you, Jaxon! It's good you have something like that."

Trying to shift the focus back to football, Ashley continued, "I guess if you're going to play a game that puts your life on the line every time you go out there, it's good to have something to believe in."

Jaxon asked, "You think so, Ashley?"

"I guess so. I mean, sure I do. Why not?"

Jaxon smiled and pushed a little more. "I'm glad to hear you say that, Ashley. I'd love to know what you believe in."

Ashley, trying to remember her previous instructions, said, "Let's get back to you. Everyone says, and I agree, that you are the greatest football player of all time. What separates you from all the greats that have played this game?"

"I don't know about that," Jaxon modestly said. "There have been some amazing players, and there are some amazing players now. I mean, Phoenix is better than I am. I don't believe my play has separated me from the greats, but from my view, how I approach the game is a little different than most."

Ashley seemed to regain her composure because the conversation had turned back to football. Jaxon had baited her back into another question, and she asked it before she even realized his plan. "How is your approach different?"

"I'm not saying others haven't done this before, but I try to keep Jesus at the forefront of every move I make. I know Jesus is rarely mentioned in college football, and if a player or coach brings Him up, others want to change the subject as quickly as possible. Even if a player or coach mentions Jesus, a skilled interviewer, like yourself, moves past the comment as if it were never mentioned. Yet if I mentioned anything else, your training would kick in, and you would ask me a follow-up question pertaining to my previous comment. You think I don't, but I pay attention sometimes."

"Let's keep this about you. This great audience didn't tune in to hear about me, Jaxon," Ashley said as she looked back into the camera with a smile on her face.

"See! There goes that reporter training again. Keep the focus where you want it. I told you! You're like a magician. Look over here!" Jaxon said as he held up his hand, pretending to shake something, while chuckling at his own joke.

"Jaxon, my business is sports. Any reporter or analyst you speak with is trying to talk to you about sports. It's not that we don't want to acknowledge you talking about your religion. It's that we want to talk about sports. You *are* college football. Our audience tunes in to us, because they want to hear about sports. Neither I nor my colleagues mean any offense to you by trying to keep the conversation relevant for our audience. Do you see why we want you to separate them?" Ashley pleaded.

"Yes, ma'am. I do," Jaxon said. "But I want you to understand why I can't separate them. That would be like trying to separate my heart from my soul. Jesus is more than just a feel-good word I throw around in an interview. I believe Jesus is the Son of God, and He came to earth to die for my sins. He did that so that I may have an eternal relationship with Him. He made it clear that if I believe in Him and confess my sins, I get to spend eternity in heaven with Him. With Jesus willing to do something like that for me, I am unwilling to separate Him from anything I do."

Ashley was taking noticeably deeper breaths, pursing her lips, and vigoursly rubbing her hands out of frustration with the direction of the conversation at this point. "That's wonderful, Jaxon. If you really think heaven is going to be that great, I hope you get to go." She said that as if she were hoping he would go sooner rather than later. "If you think He did all that for you, I can see why you would feel like you owe it to Him to bring Him up in conversation."

"Thanks, Ashley. I am excited about going. If I went today, I wouldn't be disappointed. I have been very blessed in this life, and I can't wait to bow before Him in heaven. You know what, though, Ashley?"

Ashley, sounding annoyed, asked with a sharp and unprofessional tone, "What?"

"He didn't just die for me. He died for you too. He loves you, Ashley. He paved the way to heaven for all of us. What He did He did for the entire world. He didn't do it just so we would speak highly of Him. I don't speak highly of Him because I feel like I owe Him anything. I speak highly of Him because of my love for Him. Are you at all interested in spending your eternity in heaven?"

By this point Ashley was concerned that her future as a sit-down interviewer was going down the toilet with each passing moment. She was becoming more and more agitated with Jaxon because he knew how important this was to her. She felt betrayed and wasn't happy that Jaxon seemed more interested in talking about heaven and Jesus than about helping her be successful with the interview.

Before she could stop herself, she blurted out, "Heaven isn't real. God isn't real. If heaven isn't real and God isn't real, then Jesus isn't real. I have read enough scientific information on the facts that proves heaven doesn't exist. I don't have to waste my time trying to get in there. I sure don't have any desire to go to a nonexistent place to meet a nonexisting God. I'm sorry."

Jaxon had been having these types of conversations with people since he was a child. He'd learned how to keep his cool by watching and emulating his parents while growing up. Unlike for Ashley, this conversation wasn't a frustrating one to him. He always enjoyed it when people challenged him on his beliefs because that meant there was a conversation taking place. If there was still conversation happening, it always meant the other person was still able to learn about Jesus.

"Ashley, I can see exactly where you're coming from. I can see how my beliefs seem strange or childish to those who have never felt God's presence. If I had never experienced God in the ways I have, I could see me being more skeptical too. I have noticed something in people over the years that I find very interesting. Are you willing to indulge me for a few more minutes?"

"Sure," Ashley said as she leaned back and threw her hands up, as if she had given up on her future in television.

Jaxon smiled and leaned forward in his chair again. "If I told you that when I died, I was going to go to the land of Oz to meet the Wizard, what would you think?"

Ashley wittily said, "I'm pretty sure that's what you've been telling me this whole time."

Jaxon busted out laughing. "I'm glad you've still got your sense of humor. Seriously, though, you'd think I'm crazy, right?"

"Probably," Ashley responded.

"You'd think I was crazy and possibly feel sorry for me. But you wouldn't be mad at me or spend a lot of your time and effort attempting to prove me wrong. You sure wouldn't study the subject of disproving Oz. You'd probably think I was a little off in the head and assume it wouldn't hurt anything for me to think that way, because it wouldn't affect anything."

"What's your point?" Ashley inquired.

"My point is, people don't seem to get upset about people saying crazy things that aren't realistic. They just look over them or try to get them some help. Either way, they continue to love them and try to care for them as best they know how. People are considered 'good people' if they look out for and take care of people like that."

"I'm not following you," Ashley admitted.

"Have you ever noticed how atheists and agnostics seem to get so angry with Christians about sharing their beliefs?"

Ashley gave a slight laugh and said, "No. I have no idea what you're talking about. Never experienced anything like that before. Oh wait! You mean, like right now?"

Jaxon laughed again. "Yes, ma'am. Kind of like now."

"Then, yes. I can relate," Ashley quipped.

"Great!" Jaxon exclaimed. "You know what I'm talking about then. The thing that has always seemed strange to me about atheists and agnostics is why they care in the slightest little bit about what I believe. If they truly don't believe in God, Jesus, heaven, or hell, then what does it even matter to them if I am living in la-la land? It shouldn't affect them in the slightest little bit, right? I believe I know the answer though."

Jaxon had drawn Ashley's attention by this point, and she seemed to be hanging on to his words a little longer now. "Oh yeah? What is the answer?"

"I believe the reason some people show so much animosity toward Christians is because deep inside their souls, they have an undeniable feeling of something missing in their lives. They know there is something else out there, and they can't quite explain it. They don't want to admit it, nor will they. But there is an uncomfortable feeling within them that they don't understand. God is there, and they don't like it because they don't want to sacrifice what they believe to be control of their own lives and thoughts. If they can't make sense of it, they want to crush it and destroy it."

"Well, all right," Ashley said. "Let's take your logic and turn it around. If that's the case, why do Christians care one way or another if other people believe or not? If you're going to heaven and believe it's this unbelievably great place, why do you care if other people don't want to go? That won't affect you."

"That's a great question, Ashley. That is a very good point. I have a couple of responses for you. First, it is my joy and privilege to share who God is with others. It is such an amazing thing … I want everyone to know. I am in awe that He allows me to share His word with others. I can't believe He trusts us enough to be the ones to share His message with the world. What an unbelievable opportunity!

"Second, God gave us a command to share His message with the world. We are not to keep such a great thing to ourselves. That would be very selfish and not cool. If I were given the secret to curing cancer and didn't tell others about it, you would think I was an awful person. I have news way better than any cure that will ever be created, and some people cringe when I share it. I want people to realize that Jesus is so much better than anything else I can possibly offer.

"I want to make this a little more personal though, Ashley. The reason it bothers me so much, as a Christian and as your friend, that you don't believe is because I desperately want you to experience God's love and spend your eternity in His presence. I don't want you to be away from Him for even one moment of your life. I know of a love that is so amazing. I want you to know Him the way I know Him.

"I will be in heaven, Ashley! You said it won't affect me. It *will* affect me! It will affect me profoundly if I knew that you died and never accepted Jesus's free gift of an eternal salvation. We have developed a great friendship over the years, and it would hurt me tremendously if you rejected something I was trying to share with you, especially if I knew it would save you from an eternity of literal hell.

"I've always respected you, Ashley, and I have never intentionally made you uncomfortable. I know you had a lot riding on this interview, and I do not have any desire to prevent you from being successful in your career. I will be graduating soon, and you cover college football, not pro. When I go pro, there is a good chance we will not have opportunities for interactions like we have had over the past four years. I realize that my time with you is getting shorter and shorter. I knew I would have your undivided attention today, and I didn't want to miss this precious chance to convince you. I wouldn't be able to live with myself if I didn't try harder to convince you of the truth.

"Ashley, you have such a massive following because of your heart, character, and love for those you interview. You always say you want to be more than 'just a sideline reporter.' Ashley, you are! You are an amazing person. You are beloved by sports fans everywhere, and everyone outside of sports loves you. Most importantly, you are loved by God. Jesus loves you and desperately wants a relationship with you. Ashley, God has blessed you with an amazing gift of holding people's attention, really connecting with people, and developing such a great trust with those who listen to you. I wholeheartedly believe He blessed you with your ability so you can share His word and love with others the way only you can. I really hope you will take the time to listen to that voice from within and trust what He has in store for you. It will change your life, and with your influence, you can change the lives of countless others."

When Jaxon stopped talking, Ashley sat there, completely silent. She was stunned by how far away the conversation had gone from where she originally planned. She was also trying to process all that Jaxon had said. She'd had such high hopes for this interview, and it turned out nothing like she'd anticipated. She was originally not going to be allowed to do the interview, but the producers had granted permission, because Jaxon said he would do the interview only with Ashley.

Jaxon had avoided this interview for many years. Other than pre- and post-game interactions with reporters and analysts, Jaxon had kept his distance from these formal types of interviews. He didn't like being the center of attention and preferred making the attention about his teammates. Jaxon was a great strategist. He knew that if he kept putting the interview off and keeping others desperate for the exclusive one-on-one interview, he would draw a lot more viewers. A lot more viewers meant a lot more people to hear about Jesus. Jaxon wanted the time with Ashley, because of their friendship, how she captured the hearts of millions, and his deep desire for her to become a Christian.

Ashley was certain this interview was going to ruin her career, but Jaxon was well aware of his media draw. He knew that with the amount of people projected to watch the exclusive interview, Ashley would have the perfect opportunity to gain a lot of great exposure. He assumed that if everything went according to his plan, many other networks would want access to her, and that demand would create better opportunities for her.

"Say something! Ashley, say something. We are still rolling," the yelling producer blared in Ashley's earpiece. "Get ready to go to a commercial if she doesn't recover."

"Well, there you have him, America! Jaxon Bull. The most caring and considerate man I've ever met. He's the most talented college athlete in the world, and he won't even talk about sports. He finally sits down for the interview every high-profile journalist has begged for over the last two years. He has the world's attention, and he makes the interview about me. Not only that, but he offers me his most prized possession. They broke the mold when they made him!"

# 18
## Join Me

It has been only a few minutes since Jaxon first hit the ground, but it seems like the whole world is in slow motion. Jaxon tries his best to see what is going on around him, even though he has no ability to move or speak. He can see reflections in the items around him, and all he knows is that there still seems to be a lot going on. Because Phoenix is still standing near the crowd of trainers and coaches, Jaxon can see his massive friend pacing back and forth above the crowd. Jaxon can sense the seriousness of the situation by the way everyone is behaving.

At first, nobody in the stands knows for sure who was lying on the ground. When Jaxon makes the bone-crushing hit, everyone makes the normal *Ouuuuuuuu* sound, the crowd typically makes when "The Bull" did what he had become known for doing to opposing players. Jaxon had become legendary for hitting players extremely hard and encouraging them to constantly be aware of his presence on the field. This time seemed no different. After the hit, everyone claps, cheers, and gives each other high-fives. The entire fanbase is just grateful he is on their team.

When the trainers run onto the field, the crowd gets quiet and tries to determine what happened. The video board operators are told right away, "Do not show the replay!" The crew knows it was a violent hit, and it immediately appears there is an injury that doesn't need to be seen again. Until both players are safely off the field, the video board will show only the well-known Angel mascot logo.

Tim, always in attendance for home football games, hears the crowd get quiet and immediately has a nervous feeling in his stomach. With the game in hand, he had taken a seat and proudly flipped through the pages of the game program, so he hadn't exactly seen what happened.

He is extremely excited to see this particular program, with the title "East Mississippi ANGELS, Beyond the Game" on the front cover. He can't wait to get back home and add it to his collection of Jaxon Bull memorabilia, which he has been collecting since his son's childhood. Jaxon, Tim, and Amanda are on the cover of the "senior edition" of the program. It shows the whole family with halos above their heads, and there is an article inside dedicated entirely to the family. Since Jaxon's arrival to college football as a game-changing star, all the sports channels always devoted a segment of their coverage to Jaxon, so there was little left to know about his athletic achievements. The reason this program captivates Tim's attention is that it highlights the special bond and relationships between Jaxon and Tim, Amanda, Joy, and Phoenix.

Tim is still seated and admiring the game program when he notices the crowd grow silent and everyone in the stands sits down. Tim and Amanda can sense right away that something is terribly wrong. Amanda grabs Tim's hand and squeezes tightly.

Amanda is always at the games with Tim, but her eyes are rarely on the field. Even back in Jaxon's childhood days when Jaxon was on the field, Amanda had stayed seated with her head down, praying that Jaxon wouldn't get hurt. When Jaxon wasn't on the field, she stood and cheered with the rest of the fans.

As Amanda grabs Tim's hand, he immediately stands to his feet.

The feeling he has is similar only to the day he found out about the death of his parents. By the time he gets to his feet, the training staff are already surrounding the fallen player, so he is unable to see who they were treating, but he feels it in his heart who it is. As he starts scanning for his son's number among the other players, his fears grow as he continues scanning the young men and doesn't see number eighty-nine.

His search shifts from skimming the field to being solely focused on Phoenix. Phoenix has become like a son to the Bull family due to the unbreakable bond between Phoenix and Jaxon, which has grown over the years. The Bulls are very familiar with Phoenix's story and his thoughts on having any kind of relationship with Jesus. What holds Tim's attention to Phoenix is because he sees Phoenix drop to one knee and appear to start praying.

Tim isn't the only person who notices this unique sight on the field. At the same time Tim sees Phoenix take a knee, Joy sees him as well. Immediately, Joy's right hand grabs her own left hand and starts squeezing and wringing her hands together. Because she's spent so much time around Jaxon and Phoenix, she sees Phoenix as a brother, and she knows exactly how he feels about praying. She knows Phoenix's stance on praying and kneeling to anyone or anything. Phoenix is known for his toughness and superior conditioning. Phoenix never takes a knee during a game. He never sits down during time-outs or when the team is on offense. He doesn't take breaks and never wants to be viewed as being tired or weak.

When Joy sees Phoenix drop to his knee and lower his head, as if he is praying, she knows the injury has to be worse than she feared. Upon seeing his actions, she immediately starts looking at the crowd for Tim and Amanda. The Bulls are always in the same seats, so she knows exactly where they will be.

After both Tim and Joy see Phoenix take a knee, they look directly at each other. At first, they look at each other with a combination of confusion, fear, and near panic. After seeing the fear on Joy's face while her whole body seems to be trembling, Tim realizes he and Amanda need to quickly start making their way toward the field to comfort her and get closer to their son.

Because it is senior day, both Tim and Amanda have field passes so they could be with their son as he was recognized at the beginning of the game. All the families of the seniors are on hand that day and were allowed to be on the field at the beginning of the game to share the spotlight with their sons.

Completely unbeknownst to Tim, Amanda, Joy, or Phoenix, Jaxon had a surprise in store for his closest loved ones that day. Jaxon had preplanned for Tim, Amanda, Joy, Phoenix, Andy, and BJ to all come together in the team meeting room in the athletic complex on the morning of his last home football game. He'd told his parents he wanted to do something special for Phoenix. He'd told Phoenix he wanted to do something special for Joy. He'd told Joy he wanted to do something special for his parents. He'd just told Andy and BJ to get there and enjoy a free breakfast with everyone. They all thought they were keeping secrets from one another, when in reality Jaxon was the only one with all the facts.

One week earlier, Jaxon and Phoenix were at their apartment discussing their professional football futures and having the realization that they would probably never be teammates or roommates again after the season ended. Jaxon sensed Phoenix was searching for something but would never show the kind of vulnerability it would take to have a conversation about what he was feeling.

Jaxon tried to initiate the potential conversation. "Phoenix, my brother, I'm really proud of you, dude."

Jaxon's remarks caught Phoenix off guard. "Why did you say that? Where did that come from?"

Jaxon leaned back on the couch and said, "Seriously, dude. Obviously, you have made me work my tail off in football and have made our whole team better. You have been an amazing roommate and friend to me. I know that everyone assumed you would end up getting in a lot of trouble, and Lord knows you have definitely had your chances."

"Shut up, bruh!" Phoenix shot back and started laughing.

"Seriously, though," Jaxon continued, "you have been like a brother to me, and I want you to hear that you are a good man. You need to know that you are a good man. Nobody doubts what you're gonna to do in the league, and you think that is all anyone expects of you, but I know that outside of football, you're gonna to do great things."

Phoenix, becoming uncomfortable with what Jaxon was saying, started moving around the living room. He walked over to the window, and as he was staring out, he said, "JB, I ain't you! I've been doing everything I can to stay out of trouble, but it comes easy for you. It ain't for me. I've got a fire in me! Nearly every day, I want to bust some heads. When people come at me with their stupid pens and paper, I want to knock 'em down like bowling pins. I don't have the patience you do with people. I am not a good man, and I don't know how to be, even if I wanted to be."

Jaxon tried reassuring his friend. "P. Horne, you've already become a good man, even if you didn't want to be one. You used to bring girls back to our apartment every night and talk like you weren't ever worried about hurting their feelings or getting them pregnant or if you ever saw them again. You probably thought I wasn't paying attention, but you haven't had a girl spend the night here in over a year. I haven't heard you drop *really* foul language in months. And correct me if I'm wrong, but I am pretty certain I heard you use the word *ma'am* the other day when talking to Joy."

Phoenix started laughing as he turned back toward Jaxon and said, "That was an accident."

Both Jaxon and Phoenix laughed before Phoenix continued. "That don't prove nothing. I've been in a slump."

"I don't think so!" Jaxon persisted. "You've actually become very respectful toward women and don't just see them as sexual objects, like you did when we first started living together. You go along with me now when I do community service projects. You haven't cursed in an interview in over a year. Brother, I hate to be the one to tell you, but Fish said one of the new trainers said you were 'nice' the other day."

Phoenix started laughing again and threw the football at Jaxon as he jokingly said, "Shut up!"

Phoenix grew serious again and said, "I'm not kidding, dawg. You need to lower your expectations of me. I'm not like you. Right now, I've got you to help keep me straight. I don't have a Pops like yours. Your Pops is a good man, and he taught you how to behave. I don't have a rule book telling me what I should and shouldn't be doing."

"That's where you're wrong, bro. You have access to the same book I have, but it ain't no rule book. It's a love story," Jaxon said.

"Love story? What?" Phoenix said with a confused and disgusted expression. "I ain't reading no love story."

Jaxon replied, "The book I'm talking about is God's love story to us and for us. I'm talking about a Father's love of His Son and His love for you and me. I'm talking about this." Jaxon held up his worn-out Bible and showed it to Phoenix. "The Holy Bible is God's word for us. He has given us all the directions, instructions, guidance, or whatever you want to call it we need for life. You said you don't have the kind of Pops I have, and that's where you're wrong again. Whether you realize it or not, we have the same Father. Our Father in heaven is the one who gave us all we need to be good men. Phoenix, I've already seen it in you no matter how much you deny it."

"I don't need that. I see you reading that stupid thing every day. You know that thing from cover to cover, and there can't possibly be anything else you're getting out of it. I get up in the morning, and you're reading it. I see it in your locker at practice and at games. I see it in your car. I see it with you when you come home at night. What on earth can you possibly be getting from that old book?" Phoenix asked.

"I want you to read it and find out for yourself," Jaxon replied. "I've shared the contents of this book with you over and over. I have highlighted, underlined, made notes, and practically lived inside this book since we met." As Jaxon started extending his Bible toward Phoenix, he said, "Now I want you to take this one and allow God to speak to you. I want you to allow Him in."

Phoenix put his hands up and pulled them toward himself as he backed away from Jaxon. He started walking back toward his room when he said, "Maybe some other time, dawg. I ain't ready for all that yet. I got too much fun left in me before I'm ready to be like you."

Jaxon knew the window to spend time with his friend was getting smaller with each passing day, and he was making a very bold move by offering Phoenix his Bible. Jaxon knew he had written several prayers, specifically about Phoenix, inside that Bible over the years, and he was risking their friendship if they weren't received well. He knew more importantly that Phoenix was risking his eternity if he didn't turn his life over to Jesus, so Jaxon felt the reward was worth the potential damages. Jaxon left the Bible sitting on their living room table with a note on it that said, "I am ready! HE is always ready! We are not promised tomorrow; I pray you will get ready! Your Brother, JB."

The morning of the game had arrived. Tim, Amanda, Joy, Phoenix, Andy, and BJ were all in the athletic complex, enjoying the pregame festivities. There were people everywhere. Everyone was excited about the upcoming game and talking about the potential for another national championship. There were reporters, donors, and family members scurrying all over the place. All the reporters were trying their best to elicit some emotional sound bites from the players about their last home game of the season. The game was scheduled for late that evening, so there was plenty of time before all of them had to begin their normal pregame routines.

There was one person noticeably missing from the chaos. Jaxon was already in the team meeting room, where he had been praying and preparing everything for his family and closest friends. When the time came, one by one everyone came walking into the room. They were all excited because they thought they were going to be in on some big secret, but they weren't exactly certain what the secret was they were keeping.

As they came filing into the rear entrance of the room, they spotted Jaxon standing at the front of the room with a table behind him. On the table there were five individually gift-wrapped boxes. "Good morning, everyone! Come on in and have a seat!" Jaxon announced as he pointed at the front row of the room.

Jaxon stood there with a big smile as his special guests made their way to the front and sat down in the comfortable leather seats. "Those must all be for me!" Tim exclaimed as he began lowering himself to his seat.

Amanda just shook her head and said, "Why can't you just sit down and hush?"

Jaxon nervously said, "I'm gonna go ahead and get started. Thank you all so much for joining me this morning. I have something special planned, and I can't thank you enough for helping me with all of this. I have been planning to do something special for you for quite some time now."

The group started looking at each other, trying to determine which one or ones he was talking about. None of them were being very patient because they felt they were in the dark on something about to happen.

Jaxon said, "I wanted each of you to realize how important and special you are to me, so I decided recently that instead of dragging this out, I would just do it all together. I feel like the Lord revealed to me that today was going to be a very important day for all of us and that something amazing was going to happen. I have been praying about this day for a long time now, and I feel that all of the pieces are in place for this day to turn out perfectly. Fish, come on up and get us started. I want you to grab that box and open it."

"Me?" Andy said as Jaxon pointed at the first box on the table. Andy approached the table, grabbed the gift, and said, "Why me? Are you sure?"

Andy began unwrapping the box and continued glancing around, smiling, and seemed very confused as to why he was receiving a gift. When he removed the top, he saw a roll of athletic tape, an ice pack, and some ibuprofen. He started laughing and sarcastically said, "Thanks! This is exactly what I needed. But why are you giving it to me?"

Jaxon said, "This is my last year in college, and, Lord willing, I am about to get drafted into the National Football League. I will face aches, pains, and possibly some injuries. I need my most trusted athletic trainer to join me on my journey. We have been friends since we were little, you have been with me through thick and thin, and I want you

189

to go with me to whatever team I am fortunate enough to play for in my career. I need someone caring for my injuries who I trust has my best interest in mind. Will you join me?"

Still lacking in confidence after all these years, Andy said with a slight shiver in his voice, "Are you sure you want me? There are way better trainers out there than me."

Jaxon told Andy, "You and I have been in enough battles together, I know you will always take care of me, no matter how bad the situation may get. You have watched out for me since we were kids, and I trust you with my injuries, my career, and my life. I need you on my team. Will you join me?"

Andy hugged his friend and said, "I promise I will always give you my best. Yes, I will join you. I can't wait! Thank you! Thank you! Thank you!" Everyone began clapping and congratulating Andy on getting the opportunity to be an athletic trainer in the NFL. Amanda and Joy were crying and got up to hug Andy and Jaxon.

Once Andy took his seat, Jaxon said, "BJ, come on up here, brother, and open that box."

BJ got out of his seat, walked over to Jaxon, and said, "Man, I've already got some tape." Everyone started laughing as BJ grabbed the box and began to unwrap the gift. After he opened the box, inside he saw a leather-bound planner. He reached inside, grabbed the planner, and held it up. He asked Jaxon, "Does this mean I need to get organized?"

Jaxon started laughing and responded with, "You are a man of great faith, and I have been very blessed to be part of your journey. It has been my great joy to see you help develop the men and women of FCA. You have a true calling in serving the Lord by bringing people together and developing a real sense of community among athletes. I need someone to join me on my journey who can bring my teammates and coaches together to become a united family. I need someone with a unique skill set of cockiness and humbleness that speaks to the heart of those who are used to doing things the way they want to do them. The closer we are as a team, the closer we become as a family. I want you to help me give my future family the gift of Christ. You display a relationship with Christ in a way that reaches that particular kind of group like no other person I have ever met. Will you join me?"

For the first time ever, BJ stood silent before Jaxon without a quick and witty comeback. He extended his hand toward Jaxon and said, "I never told you this, but I'm glad you didn't go to Belmont."

They both started laughing and hugged one another. "Does that mean you'll join me?" Jaxon inquired.

"Yes! I'm in," BJ replied.

Jaxon turned and looked at Phoenix. "You're next, big guy. Come on up."

As BJ took his seat, Phoenix got out of his and walked slowly toward the table. He saw the box with his name on it, and as he pointed at the gift, he asked, "What's in there?"

Jaxon then slid Phoenix's box to the other side of the table and said, "We will get to that in a minute." He turned to his parents and said, "Mom, Dad, come on up here please." Tim shot out of his chair and immediately started searching for a box with his name on it, while Amanda tried to settle him down.

"Hold on, Dad, you'll get to open one in a minute," Jaxon reassured Tim.

Jaxon turned back to Phoenix and said, "My brother, you and I have been challenging one another, helping each other grow, and alongside one another since day one. We have battled on and off the field, and there is no gridiron warrior out there I would rather have by my side on Saturdays. There is no other roommate I would have rather lived with in my time here. I know your blood family will not be on the field with you today, but I ask that you do me and my family the honor of standing with us today. You are my brother. You are our blood. My mom and dad see you as a son, and as far as we are concerned, you are our family. Will you join me?"

Phoenix stood silently and stared at the floor for a minute. He didn't know what to say and didn't want to appear to need anyone or anything. He was strong and proud. He had been a loner and was firm in his abilities to make it on his own. Amanda was the first to move. She was already in tears as she walked over to Phoenix. She didn't say a word. She put her arms around him and hugged him. She was holding him tightly as she reached for Jaxon and pulled him in close.

As she stared into Phoenix's eyes, she said, "You are my son, and I would be hurt if you didn't stand with us. I couldn't be a prouder mother of my two amazing boys!" Because they had spent so much time together over the years, she knew the best way to get Phoenix to join them on the field for senior day was to seem as if she needed him more than he needed them.

"Momma Bull," Phoenix said, "if it means that much to you, I can't turn you down. Y'all have been so good to me. I wouldn't think of hurting your feelings."

With that response, Tim walked over to shake Phoenix's hand and give him a hug. He grabbed Jaxon too and said, "I'm proud of you boys. I'm proud of how y'all watch out for each other and have helped each other become men. Bless me silly. I'm proud of all of you kids." Tim pointed to Joy, Jaxon, Phoenix, Andy, and BJ. "Momma, I think they all took after me! Don't you?"

"They didn't get your humbleness," Amanda said.

At this point, Joy was in tears, and she started hugging everyone and was trying to keep her composure.

"What's in my box?" Phoenix asked.

"You know what it is. It's the gift I've offered you plenty of times over the years, and you've yet to be ready for it. It's here, and it's the best gift I could offer you. It's everything you need to find your way as we move forward in life. This gift is yours, and it is ready for you when you are ready for it." Phoenix just nodded and put the box under his arm. The others were curious, but nobody asked.

"We've got a little bit more to go. Y'all take your seats." As everyone started back to the seats, Jaxon said, "Mom. Dad. Y'all hold up."

Tim spun back around and said, "My turn! I'm ready to open my present!" When he got back to the table, he saw the gift was labeled, "Mom Only!" Tim appeared so disappointed when he didn't see anything with his name on it. He said, "You misspelled 'Awesome Dad'" as he pointed toward the box.

Jaxon said, "Turn the card over."

Tim flipped over the card that said, "Mom Only!" and saw on the back side where it said, "Just kidding. Mom AND Dad." Tim looked up and said, "That's dirty!" and handed the box to Amanda. He said to her, "My dear, would you like to do the honors?"

As Amanda stared at Jaxon, she was still wiping her eyes. "I don't know if I can handle any more of these. I can't stop crying. This whole thing is too sweet and emotional for me."

Tim reached for the box and said, "I can open it."

Amanda pulled the box back toward her and said, "I can do it."

She opened the box and immediately started crying when she saw what was inside. With one hand she held the box, and with the other she covered her mouth. She set the box down and reached inside to slowly and carefully pull out the contents. Inside was the senior edition of the football program. The picture on the cover was of Amanda and Tim in their prime, with halos superimposed above them. Both were in great shape and were holding Jaxon when he was about five years old, wearing a tiny black-and-red East Mississippi Angels football uniform. Amanda couldn't say a word. She just kept crying as she admired the cover.

Tim put his arm around Amanda to comfort her, and he took hold of the other side of the magazine. They were both admiring the old picture of the young family, and Tim said, "That's really something, Son. How'd you get them to do that?" He continued staring at it as he took a deep breath to keep from tearing up and said again, "That's really something."

"Mom, Dad, you have been my inspiration my entire life. You have molded me and shaped me into the man I am today. You instilled a love for Christ in me by the way you loved each other and served the Lord, our family, our community, and everyone you've ever come in contact with. I have been blessed beyond measure with you as my parents, my coaches, and my friends. I can never repay what you have done for me, but it is you who deserve the credit for what I have accomplished.

"Dad, you taught me to work harder than anyone else, to never quit, and always to have a sense of humor. Mom, you showed me what it was like to put others first and always to serve the Lord in everything I do. The way you two have loved each other over the years has made me want to be the best man I can be. I get credited all the time for my good character, and all these reporters say how I have set the bar for the way college football players should behave, but it is you who have set the bar. This interview is mostly about you and how selfless you have been for your entire lives. You are the best people I know, and I couldn't have asked for better parents. You mean the world to me, and I can never thank you enough. I love you so much, and I am grateful for you. Thank you for joining me today and for loving my friends so well."

The whole group was on their feet, standing around the table, admiring the program, and hugging again. Phoenix was being the quiet one of the bunch because he was uncomfortable around love and affection, but he was more comfortable around Jaxon's family than around anyone else in his life. Tim had a way about him that made everyone feel welcome, and Amanda always made everyone feel special and loved. Phoenix, Andy, and BJ had become honorary children of

Tim and Amanda as soon as they came into Jaxon's life. They always treated all of Jaxon's friends like they were their own kids.

"All right, I've got one more to go. Everyone, take a seat," Jaxon said as he took a big, deep breath. He waited for everyone to sit back down before he began. He walked over to Joy, reached for her hand, and said, "You're up, young lady!"

Joy, with tears still in her eyes from all the other moments that had already taken place, reached for Jaxon's hand. He pulled her to her feet and walked her back to the table. "So far, this has been an amazing morning with everyone, and I am so fortunate to have you here sharing it with us. Joy, you have been and continue to be an inspiration to me, and I can't thank you enough for taking a chance on me. I know you still don't believe me, but I still thank the Lord every day that He blessed me with the most amazing woman ever. I am known for being a big, strong guy, but around you I feel like a lovesick puppy. My time with you has been the most enjoyable time of my life. I am a better man because of you. I know you said the words 'I love you' were going to be reserved for your husband, so we have withheld those words from one another our entire relationship. You mean more to me than I will ever be able to express with three short words anyway. With everything I had planned for everyone today, I wouldn't feel right having this moment with everyone else and not offering you something special too," Jaxon said as he motioned toward the gift on the table.

Joy was paralyzed. She just stood there, staring at the box. She loved Jaxon more than she had ever loved anyone in her entire life. Over the course of their relationship, she had finally become more comfortable with how much he loved her, but she still couldn't understand why he did. She had been scarred and, in her mind, damaged. It was difficult for her to trust, and Jaxon had worked night and day to try to earn her trust. She knew Jaxon was a godly man. She knew he could love others, regardless of whether other people felt the ones he loved were worthy of his love. Regularly she wrestled over whether she deserved to be loved by him, but it never changed how she felt about him. She also believed he could have any girl in the world and always wondered why he had chosen one as damaged as her.

Joy reached for the box and slowly unwrapped the gift. Once she got the box unwrapped, she carefully lifted the lid. Once she had the lid off, she leaned forward and peeked inside the box. Her eyes immediately went from being tear filled, her hands being jittery, to having an expression of panic on her face. She spun around and shouted, "It's empty!" After she turned all the way around, she saw Jaxon down on one knee, holding a ring box.

Jaxon opened the box and said, "Joy, you are the love of my life. I love you very much! I have loved you since the first time I saw you. None of what I have shared today would be complete without you. Will you join me?"

Joy lost her look of panic and started crying again. She dropped to her knees, started hugging Jaxon, and said, "I love you, Jaxon! I love you so much. I can't believe this!"

Jaxon leaned back, grabbed Joy by her shoulders, and asked, "Is that a yes?"

"Yes!" Joy exclaimed. "Yes! I will join you anywhere!"

# 19
## Mission Accomplished

It is getting more difficult for Jaxon to keep his eyes open. He is becoming very tired and is ready to stand up, but he still can't move. Fish is still in his face, still trying to provide words of encouragement to his fallen friend. Andy hasn't budged since he first placed his hands around Jaxon's helmet.

Andy has his sunglasses on top of his head, and Jaxon realizes he can see a lot of what is going on in the reflection of the lenses. He sees his friend BJ leading a prayer with a group of the players on the sidelines. This is such a comforting sight to Jaxon because he clearly remembers BJ coming to know Christ and the fond memories he has of them growing closer together over the years.

He can see Phoenix doing something he knows can only be an act of God. Seeing Phoenix down on his knee and the fact that he appears to be praying makes him smile and think back on the conversation they had the year before about the draft.

Because of Phoenix's love for his team and the competitiveness with Jaxon, he ended up not going pro his junior season. After deciding to stay in college, he set his sights on Jaxon's spot in the draft. Phoenix was bound and determined to become the number one draft pick and go ahead of Jaxon. He felt like he would be cheated of the chance to beat Jaxon in the draft if he went pro his junior year and Jaxon didn't go until his senior year.

Seeing Jaxon lying on the field, Phoenix realized his friend would never play football again. At that moment, it dawned on him what he had said their junior year, believing at the time that there was no conceivable way it could happen. *If I go ahead of you in the draft, it will prove to me that God exists. I will drop to my knees at that very moment and give my life to Him.*

There is a lot of anger in Phoenix, and he scares a lot of people. Nobody ever messes with him, and many fear him, but with all his negative qualities, Phoenix is a man of his word.

Phoenix drops to his knee and begins to pray. "God, I'm here. I know now that You are real. You don't have to do this. I don't have to go first in the draft to believe. Get him up! I am in. I will join You. Don't take my friend. Don't take my brother. Jesus, please keep him safe and protect my boy. I give myself to You, and I pray that You will come into my heart and make me at least half the man Jaxon is. Jaxon has told me about You for years, but I want to know You for myself. I want to love You the way he loves You. Lord, I will do what You want. I will do my part. Lord, make him get up!"

By this time, Tim and Amanda have made their way down to the sidelines. Amanda can see Joy is holding on to her engagement ring like she is afraid it is going to disappear. Her face has no color in it, and she appears terrified. Amanda puts her arms around Joy, and Tim holds them both.

Jaxon shifts his eyes from Phoenix and can now see the cheerleaders. They are all down on a knee, and many of them appear to be praying. Jaxon knows Joy has to be close, so he continues searching until he sees her and his parents together. They are all holding each other and seem to be trying to comfort each other. As Jaxon continues looking around, he sees more and more people praying. He knows the situation doesn't look good for him, but he is extremely excited to see such a large amount of people praying. That is certainly not a familiar sight at a college football game, and he loves and cherishes every moment of it.

"Roll the video!" the man in charge of the video board shouts out to the crew working the jumbotron.

"What video?" one of the workers shouts back.

"Play Jaxon's team captain video for senior day," the man in charge insists. "We need to find something to keep everyone calm. This doesn't appear to be good."

"We aren't supposed to run those until the end of the game," another scoreboard operator chimes in.

"Only show Jaxon's," the first man says. "Get it ready and play it!"

The video board comes on with a close-up shot of Jaxon sitting on a stool in a dark room with a bright light pointed directly at him. "Good evening!" Jaxon starts his speech. Every eye in the stands and, with the exception of the medical staff, on the field and sidelines is locked in on the massive screen.

"It's been a great four years!" Jaxon continues. "I can't believe how time flies. We have been through a lot together, and I have cherished every moment of it. You are the best fans in the country, and I consider myself very blessed to be an East Mississippi Angel. Both figuratively and literally. You have loved me and my family very well. We have been incredibly blessed to be a part of this community. Regardless of where my journey takes me, my mom, dad, and Joy are forever East Mississippi Angels. Aside from an amazing run in football, the more impactful experience for me has been serving this community and getting to know each of you. I can't thank you enough for your support on mission trips, community projects, prayer groups, and other aspects of serving, in which you have partnered with me over the years. I pray that, even after I am gone, you will continue what we have started.

"I love you, and I pray that each of you will come to know our Lord, Jesus Christ. I have never been shy about my faith, and I pray that He has been glorified in all you have seen in me. Please do not just see me as an accomplished athlete but as a man who tries his best to serve the God he loves. I pray that you will see that my life has been more than just jerseys, trophies, wins, and ticket sales. It is my prayer that no matter what you believe, you will always seek the Truth and never stop loving and being kind to one another.

"If you will allow me, I ask that you indulge me in one last, selfish favor. Tonight, is my last night on this field as a player. I will be declaring for the NFL draft soon, and my teammates and I will be going our separate ways in life. My goal is, and has always been, to love others well and lead as many people to Christ as I can. Even if football were to end for me today, my purpose will not change. The conduit in which I fulfill my purpose may change, but my purpose will remain.

"I ask that you pray for my teammates and me. Even if you aren't someone who prays, please join hands with those sitting next to you and offer us some positive and encouraging thoughts. Please pray that we will live well, serve well, and love well no matter where we end up. I ask that you pray for my family and, more specifically, for my beautiful girlfriend and hopefully by now my fiancée, Joy Battle. If today goes as I have planned, this will be the best day of my life. There are so many here tonight who have had such an amazing impact on my life, and I am blessed beyond what I could have ever deserved. I have had an amazing run here, both literally and figuratively. My time here has come to an end, but I am ready for the next step. Regardless of where I end up, you will forever be in my heart. Go, Angels, and God bless!"

At the conclusion of Jaxon's speech, you could hear a pin drop in the stadium.

*Thump thump …*

With the silence that now fills the air, Jaxon can hear his heart beating again.

*Thump thump …*

All begin to hold hands and bow their heads. Jaxon can see that Andy's eyes are squeezed closed and full of tears. He fixes his eyes on Andy's sunglass lenses again, and everyone he can see appears to be holding hands and praying, just as he has requested.

Jaxon's breathing begins to slow down tremendously, and he has an astonishing calm about him. He had no idea that the words in his video were going to fit so well to the unfortunate situation he is in, but he is incredibly grateful to see so many people praying on his behalf.

He can see his parents and Joy holding one another. He can tell they are praying, and he feels so blessed to have those three amazing people in his life. He knows God has blessed him in such tremendous ways, and it has never been as apparent to him as it is in this moment.

*Thump thump …*

Andy can tell Jaxon's breathing has slowed down to the point that it is nearly nonexistent. He slowly opens his eyes to see whether Jaxon is still awake.

*Thump thump …*

"Don't you give up! Don't give up, Bull. Hang in there! The stretcher is here. We're going to get you out of here and get you some help!"

*Thump thump …*

Jaxon never says a word. With no expression of panic or fear, he stares directly into Andy's eyes. He realizes he has said everything he wanted to say to his most cherished loved ones that day. He has been fortunate enough to tell the entire crowd and the world about Jesus. He's witnessed the toughest guy he knows drop to his knees and accept Jesus as his Lord and Savior. His fiancée and his best friends love his family, and his family loves them more than he could have ever hoped for. He knows that regardless of whether he ever gets up from this field, he is very blessed, and God is good. He has a peace about him that he has never felt before. He knows this is the perfect day.

*Thump thump …*

Jaxon, never breaking eye contact with Andy, takes a big, deep breath and slowly smiles.

*Thump … thump …*

*Thump.*

# About the Author

P.S. Harper writes from the heart and experiences of being raised in a small southern town. A Mississippi native, he grew up poor in an unstable environment, not knowing his father until he was in his 30's. The only father figure he knew was the alcoholic stepfather that married his encouraging mother, who was in and out of their lives until he was 15 years old. After developing a relationship with Christ as a young adult, Harper completely supported himself through college. With his love of sports and recreation, he earned a master's degree from Ole Miss in 2004. Upon graduating, Harper worked for the University of Alabama for six years; mentoring, teaching, and developing students. He currently works at Auburn University serving one of the premier Campus Recreation departments in the country. Harper has spent his entire life attempting to be a blessing to others.